AMBER OAK

MYSTERIES

Volume 2

By
Ceara Comeau

Published by Lulu.com

ISBN 978-1-257-95493-3

Table of Contents

The Tragedy of Tear Drop Island

Chapter 1

A Wonderful Surprise

"Wow! I can't believe it! I'm finally going to see my cousins all the way over in Germany! I wonder if they still remember me!" exclaimed Amber to herself as she looked out the window of the plane.

The loudspeaker came on and the pilot announced something first in German, then French, and finally in English, "Ladies and gentlemen, please fasten your seat belts. We are coming in for a landing!" Everyone did as the pilot asked and the plane made a swift descent making the landing very smooth.

Amber looked out her window and saw much fog. The airport was incredibly large and fancy for the city she was in but nonetheless she got off the plane. The inside of the airport was very pristine, but there was only one problem, she didn't know enough German to be able to identify where the conveyor belt was! As she was searching for her luggage she wondered to herself, "Where are Brendan and Andrea? I hope they can find me with all these people around."

As she pushed through crowds of people, Amber eventually found the conveyor belt and searched for her navy blue bags. While looking, she noticed others around her taking strange glimpses at her. "Great, I'll be known as a weirdo here as well," she whispered to herself. When she retrieved her bags, she went off to search for her family. However, she didn't have to search long for within a minute she heard someone yelling, "Amber, Amber! We are over here!"

1

Amber pushed through the crowd of people and saw a tall young man waving his hands towards her. She looked to her cousin, Brendan, who was now seventeen and very tall. He was tan and had dark brown hair. His hazel eyes seemed like they penetrated you as soon as you looked into them. He was also very lean and had a deep voice. Andrea stood right beside him and she was fifteen (a year younger than Amber). She was a bit smaller than Brendan, but she was outgoing and spunky just like Amber. Andrea's appearance was different than her brother. She had dark, liquid brown eyes and light brown hair. She was lean, too.

"We are so glad you could come!" said Andrea with a heavy German accent.

"Agreed!" replied Amber.

"The car is waiting, let us hurry we have so much to show you today!" exclaimed Brendan.

They led Amber out of the airport and to their car, which was a red convertible.

"Let me take your bags," offered Brendan as soon as they reached the car.

Amber got into the car and looked at all of her surroundings. There were few trees and the airport had many windows. She took one last glimpse of the area then jumped in the car. Brendan turned down the top of the convertible and Amber leaned back, shut her eyes, and let the wind blow her long, shiny dark brown hair, as they drove off. After a few moments, she opened her eyes and looked around. They were driving on a narrow paved road that had a large hill to the left and a wide river to the right. The scenery was so beautiful to Amber it was perfect. They took a turn off the road and went up the hill. The car kept climbing and climbing without hesitation, and then it finally reached the top. Amber sat up and looked around. It was a much better view. There were no trees at all and she could see a large lake below. The view went away as the car drove down the hill. The road had many twists and sharp turns but then after a while they finally reached a beautiful large white house. It had black shutters and a brick chimney to the side. There was a garage, which was built off to the side of the house near where the grass and the forest met. Behind the house, Amber caught a glimpse of the large lake. Out in the water was a diving dock. The shore was small and rocky. The car came to a halt and Amber got out of the car. "Am I in heaven?" asked Amber.

Andrea laughed and replied, "I guess you could say that it is a heaven on earth. Let me take your bags."

Andrea and Brendan led Amber into the house. The inside of the house was much larger than it first appeared. There was a large staircase with a black banister and there were many bright colored rooms. They walked up the stairs and stopped by the first door on their left.

"This is your room, Amber. I hope you find it comfortable," said Andrea entering the room and putting the luggage down.

The room was also very bright. The walls were yellow and there was a light wood floor with a fancy white carpet in the center of the room. The bed frame was golden and the bedspread matched the carpet.

Amber went downstairs and went into the living room. From there she could see the beautiful lake. An hour later, Brendan and Andrea came in and Andrea said, "Amber, would you like to get a better view of the lake?"

"Definitely!" replied Amber following Brendan and Andrea out the door. Once they got outside Amber was led down a little pathway and ended up at the edge of the lake. She peered out over the vast body of water and was amazed at its beauty. Birds flew overhead and the trees across the lake swayed in the breeze and there was a distant sound of kids playing in the water.

"Wow, this place is incredible!!" exclaimed Amber.

The other two smiled and Brendan replied, "We thought you would like it! Maybe tomorrow we can go for a swim."

"Why couldn't we go now?" asked Amber.
Brendan glanced at his watch and replied, "It is six o'clock right now and it will be dark very soon. Plus, mother is making a special dinner tonight."

3

It seemed like a good enough excuse to Amber so she followed her cousins back into the house, before she entered, she looked back at the picture perfect lake and sighed, "I wish I could be able to wake up to this beauty every day."

Chapter 2

The Crystal

The next morning Amber awoke to the smell of bacon, eggs, and coffee. She put on her bathrobe and walked down stairs. She followed the wonderful smells to the kitchen and found her Aunt Loralee making coffee and her Uncle Henry making breakfast. She walked over to the table and sat next to Brendan.

"Good morning, Amber! What would you like to eat?" asked Uncle Henry.

"Well, I'd like eggs and bacon if you don't mind," replied Amber stifling a yawn.

"Absolutely, coming right up," he replied.

As Amber waited for her food, Andrea spoke up and said, "Okay, we have a big day ahead of us. After breakfast, go get dressed and we will head out and go shopping in town!"

Amber liked that idea and after she ate she ran upstairs and got changed. Now, Amber wasn't the type of girl who loved shopping but this was an exception; after all, she was in a different country.

She ran back down the stairs and saw her cousins by the car. She ran outside and asked, "Where do we go now?"

"Now, we shop!!" exclaimed Andrea getting into the car. They went off out of the countryside and eventually tall buildings started to appear over the horizon. As they started getting closer to the city Amber noticed that the buildings and other surroundings weren't as different as she thought they'd be. In fact the only thing that was different was the titles of the buildings.

Brendan parked the car and everyone jumped out and headed towards the stores. The girls went into every clothing and jewelry store they could find. Amber got a few clothes and some jewelry. Then the time came where they had to meet up and get lunch.

They found Brendan in a video game store and they decided where they were going to eat. The three teens walked down the street and entered into a small café.

"So, I see at least one of you girls have definitely done a lot of shopping," said Brendan looking at his sister.

"Yes, well, we both did and we had loads of fun, right, Amber?"

"I have to agree with you, Andrea!"

The teens sat down and ordered lunch, and as they were eating Brendan said to Amber, "How about after lunch we go for a little hike in the woods. I know of a fantastic place to hike, and Amber, I am sure you will love the view! Then later on we can go for a swim!"

"That'd be great!" she replied with enthusiasm.

They finished their lunch and paid for it, and then they were off on another adventure...

Amber found the woods enthralling. It had never occurred to her how beautiful it could be! There were a lot of trees, all of different shapes and sizes. The sun shining through them made it appear to be almost surreal. The wonderful smells filled Amber's nose.

"There are no words to describe how amazing this is!" exclaimed Amber, who seemed in a far off world.

"We knew you would love it, Amber!" replied Andrea with a little laugh.

Soon this breathtaking wood came to an end and the trio entered into an area that had flowers on both sides of the trail. Amber couldn't decide which was more beautiful... the woods or this forest of flowers. "Wow! I've never seen anything like this before! So many different colors!" exclaimed Amber in surprise.

She had a very good reason to be surprised. These two fields of flowers were nothing that could be found in America. There were red flowers, yellow, orange, green blue, pink, yellow, white, teal, baby blue, few black, and multi-colored!"

This scenery couldn't help but make Amber smile! She almost didn't want to leave! Well that is, until Brendan said, "Amber, would you like to go for a swim now?"

Amber nodded and they headed back through the woods and to the car to drive back home.

They returned home, got on their bathing suits and ran to the water. Amber dipped her toe into the water and jumped back. "Oh my gosh! This water is freezing!!!!" she exclaimed.

"It is, but it will take awhile getting used to," said Andrea laughing.

Andrea was right. Little by little the teens stepped a bit further into the water. Eventually they all were jumping around and splashing each other.

"I'm going to dive and see if there's anything on the lake floor," announced Andrea.

The other two nodded and Andrea started her little investigation.

Andrea was an excellent swimmer and could swim under water for quite a long time.

The underwater world held much beauty. There were many varieties of fish, a sandy bottom floor and if you looked up you could see the sun gleaming through the surface giving it a crystal-like appearance.

As Andrea was swimming something shiny caught her eye. She dove down further to take a closer look. She picked it up and it appeared to be a lavender colored crystal. She thought it was the oddest thing. She had never seen anything like it. She swam up to the surface and went to shore.

"Hey, guys, look what I found!" exclaimed Andrea.

Brendan and Amber rushed over to see Andrea's discovery.

"Wow! That is a strange crystal. I wonder what kind it is?" said Brendan.

Amber took the crystal and examined it.

"I don't know, either," she admitted.

The three went back to their towels and let the sun dry them off. As Andrea put the crystal in the sun, the shimmer the crystal set off mesmerized her.

Amber sat on her towel and leaned back so the sun could warm her up from the cold water. She sat up and looked back toward the lake and examined her surroundings. She again caught eye of the small island in the middle of the lake. Finally, the island got the better of her curiosity and she asked, "Brendan? What's that island over there in the distance?"

A grim look spread across his face and he replied, "Nobody knows the real name of it, but everyone around here calls it Tear Drop Island."

"Why?" asked Amber.

Andrea spoke up and replied, "It is because it has a very tragic tale. Apparently a well-known family lived there during the 1930's. There was a mother, father, sister, and brother. The girl's name was Adelina and she was the prettiest thing you had ever seen. Then there was her brother Adalard who was very strong and helped his father out around the house. One night, some Nazis burned down their house and Adelina attempted to save her family but it was too late. Plus, she barely escaped with her life!"

"Wow, that's a great story, Andrea! But how do you know it's true and why would they burn down their house?" asked Amber.

"First of all, these people were Jews and secondly Germany knows it is true!" said Brendan.

"Have you actually been over there to investigate the island?" questioned Amber.

"No, nobody goes over there anymore, at least not since the fire. Why are you so interested in the island anyway?" asked Andrea.

"Well, you see, back in America I'm known for solving mysteries. You know, an amateur detective," Amber replied shyly.

"That is pretty cool, Amber! I am sorry to say there is no mystery on Tear Drop Island though," said Andrea.

"Well, you never know," said Amber hopefully. Brendan saw Amber's smile fade, but then he replied,

"Maybe we could go over to the island sometime."

"I'll look forward to that," said Amber.

The three teens went back into the water and swam for a bit longer then went back to the house, for Aunt Loralee announced that dinner was almost ready. When Amber was dressed she went to the windowsill and waited for dinner. She looked out and noticed that she had a perfect view of the lake including Tear Drop Island. She stared at the island for some time and then thought to herself, "Something isn't right with this island...I can't say for sure what that is, but I believe there is much more to its history than meets the eye."

Chapter 3

A Weird Discovery

That night, as everyone went to bed, Amber had a terrible dream. She had dreamt about the story her cousin had told her about Tear Drop Island! The nightmare woke the young sleuth up. She looked around and then looked at the clock. "I'll go back to sleep and maybe I won't have the dream again!" said Amber to herself.

The next time Amber woke up it wasn't from the nightmare, but from the sound of a loud banging against her bedroom door. Amber sat up, rubbed her eyes and stretched, "Who is it?" she asked in a tired voice.

"Amber, can I come in? It is Andrea," replied the excited girl.

Amber got up and opened the door. The young girl was jumping up and down and then gave Amber a big hug. "Andrea, what's wrong?" asked Amber slightly befuddled.

"Guess what!? You, Brendan and I are going to Addie's House. It is a historical landmark in our town. I have been wanting to go there for a very long time!" said Andrea.

Amber couldn't help but laugh at her cousin's excitement. "When are we leaving?" asked Amber.

"We are leaving at eleven o'clock, but I must go now and get ready!" she replied as she raced down the hall into her room.

Amber went to the closet and pulled out one of the new outfits that she got yesterday. After she got dressed she looked at her bedside clock and saw that it was already 10:30. "Oh my goodness! I haven't even had breakfast yet!" she exclaimed as she rushed out the door.

Amber flew down the stairs and came to an abrupt stop. She almost ran into her Uncle Henry who was holding a mug of steaming hot coffee in one hand and a newspaper in the other. "Oh! I am so sorry, Uncle Henry, it's just Andrea told me that I should hurry and get ready for our little adventure today," said Amber apologetically.

Uncle Henry turned around and looked at his daughter. Andrea's cheeks turned a light pink and replied, "Sorry, dad."

Uncle Henry smiled and replied, "It is okay, sweetheart. Now, if you kids will excuse me I must get back to the morning news."

As soon as he left the room, Andrea got up and said, "It is eleven o'clock now. Let's go!"

"But I haven't had breakfast yet!" said Amber.

Andrea rushed over to the counter, grabbed a muffin and handed it to Amber.

"Andrea, how did you know that I liked chocolate chip muffins?"

"A little birdie told me, now we must hurry!" she replied.

Andrea quickly stopped before she got in the car and then exclaimed, "Wait! I need to get my gem, I left it on the kitchen counter!" exclaimed Andrea.

"Andrea? Are you sure you want to bring it? It might get lost," called Brendan.

"No, it will not get lost. I turned it into a ring!" replied the girl coming out of the house and showing off her new treasure.

"Well, that is a very creative idea, Andrea," said Amber. Andrea smiled and they all got into the car and off they went.

"So, tell me more about the place that we're going to," said Amber.

"Remember how I told you about how we are going to Addie's house? Well, she was a hero during World War II. She rebelled against the Nazis and she also took many refugees into her home. She later died because of some sort of sickness," explained Andrea.

Amber soaked up all of this information. She thought that this would be an exciting adventure. After a while of driving up and down hills and turning around sharp corners they finally reached their destination.

The house was completely made of stone and it was set on top of a hill. There were many tall trees surrounding it and an old-fashioned well was a little ways away.

"Wow, this place is incredible!" said Amber as she stepped out of the car, "How often do people come here?"

"Well, actually, the owner of this building does not allow many people to come here. He is afraid that someone will vandalize the house," said Brendan.

"Then how were you able to get permission to visit?" asked Amber.

"We know the owner and we told him that we would like to see Addie's house. He said it was fine with him," said Andrea.

As the three kids went to the house, Amber noticed the colorful birds flying through the trees and she heard a faint trickle of a small brook near the house. Brendan took out a shiny key and unlocked the door and all three went in.

On the inside there was a round table in the center of the room. There were many shelves and most if not all of them appeared to have some sort of glass on them. The teens searched through the small house and after a while Brendan announced, "Hey look at this! I believe it is the storage room Addie used to store food for the refugees!!"

Andrea went into the storage room and looked around. The only things she saw were a few broken jars and several layers of shelves. When she came out she said, "Boy, I wish that we could see what it was like in her time!" Just as she said that, Andrea's ring began to glow!

"Um, guys where did you go?" asked Andrea after a few moments.

"Andrea, we are right here," said Brendan.

"I can here you but I cannot see you!" said Andrea almost in tears, "Can you see me?"

"Yes, we can. Now, Brendan, hold Andrea's hand and tell me what you see," said Amber. Brendan made his way over to Andrea and took hold of her hand.

"Oh my! Amber, where did you go?" asked Brendan. Amber ignored Brendan's question and asked, "Andrea, can you now see your brother?"

"Yes, but we cannot see you! What is going on?" she asked crying.

"I'll tell you in a minute," replied Amber.

"Oh my word! Is that... is that Addie?" asked Brendan who now appeared scared.

Amber rushed over to Brendan's side and grabbed his hand. In that moment the scenery changed around her. It was a bit darker outside, a fire was going in the stone fireplace, food was cooking on the stove, and a woman was bringing refugees into the house. She motioned them all to sit down and she poured each of them a bowl full of soup. Amber felt around in her pocket for a pen and a piece of paper. When she got them out she wrote something down and handed it to Andrea.

"Andrea, read this," said Amber. Andrea did as she was told and said, "It is now time for me to say; bring me back from whence I came."

The scenery of Addie with her refugees slowly faded into the distance and the modern day scenery came into view.

"Amber, I think you had better tell us what is going on," said Brendan in his most serious voice.

Amber shyly nodded and explained to them what had happened. "Well, that gem that you found, Andrea, isn't really a gem. It's actually the smallest star ever recorded. It's called the Time Travel Star and it only comes once every seven hundred years. It looks like a normal shooting star, well, until it hits earth. Not only that, but it chooses where it wants to go! Only the person who found the star (he or she is called the star bearer) can control the star. If you're in a place and you want to see what happened in the past all you need to do is tell it what you want to see and when you want the vision to end the star bearer has to say:

"It is now time for me to say; bring me back from whence I came."

The people and animals cannot see you when you are in the past. The downer about it is that you only get two wishes. It looks like you have one left because if you used all your wishes the gem wouldn't be lavender anymore, it'd look like a diamond. So, I'd suggest you'd save your last wish for something really important."

"I will, but how did you know this?" asked Andrea.

"Well, I read about it online a while back, but I thought it was just a myth! Trust me, I was just as shocked as you guys were," said Amber.

"Well, let us go home. I think we have had enough time travel for one day," said Brendan turning towards the door.

Chapter 4

Tear Drop Island

When they all arrived back home, they decided to eat dinner on the back porch.

"Amber, we have another surprise for you," said Andrea smiling. "What is it?" asked Amber.

"Well, Andrea and I have decided to bring you over to Tear Drop Island so you could do your "investigating," said Brendan.

"Really? Are you serious?" asked Amber in obvious excitement. "

I do not see why we could not, it is still light out and it will be by the time we return," stated Andrea. So, after dinner, the teens got a canoe out of the garage and made their way to the water. Once all were settled in Brendan and Andrea took the oars and paddled their way to the island.

As they got closer and closer the island looked more and more menacing. Amber, in fact, started having second thoughts about going to the island, but it was too late to turn around now, they had already reached the shore.

Brendan started paddling toward the dock but then Amber spoke up and said, "I wouldn't go near the dock if I were you." "Why?" asked Brendan.

"Well, it doesn't look that safe. Why don't we tie it up to a tree," she replied.

"Do we have a rope?" questioned Brendan.

Amber looked around in the boat and said, "No, we don't."

"On the contrary, I picked up some rope on the way out of the garage. It never hurts to be prepared," said Andrea, holding a thick woven rope.

Brendan smiled at his little sister, got out and tied the boat up. Then he helped the girls out.

"This is a really small island," said Andrea looking around. The trio walked farther onto the island and eventually came across a little house.

"I thought you guys said that the house burned down," said Amber, looking at them.

"We thought so too," replied Andrea who looked confused.

"Well, that goes to show you that you can't believe everything you hear," said Amber. The teen sleuth walked off toward the house and the other two followed her.

"Whoa! What happened in here?" asked Amber as she stepped through the doorway. There were glass shards all over the place! Chairs were overturned. It looked like a hurricane came through!

"So, if the legend is not true, then what really did happen here?" asked Brendan. Andrea looked down at her ring and said, "There is only one way to find out."

"Andrea, are you sure? I mean, do you really want to?" asked Brendan.

Andrea nodded and replied, "Brendan, hold my hand and Amber, hold his." They did as Andrea said and she continued, "I wish we could find out what happened here."

Once again the scenery changed. It was dark outside and four new people were inside the house. There was the man and a woman and then two young teens that everyone assumed were Adelina and Adalard.

"Brendan, can you translate what they're saying?" asked Amber. Brendan nodded.

Suddenly the door flew open and in came two German soldiers! Adelina was the first to see them and she hid as soon as possible. The two soldiers grabbed Adalard and his father. The mother screamed and charged at the soldiers. One of them raised a gun and shot her. She fell to the ground with a loud thump. She was dead. The other soldier started talking and Brendan translated.

"You will come with us, we need more strong men!"

"Please, let us be! Please!" cried Adalard.

"Silence! Do you have any other family members?" demanded the other soldier. All was quiet.

"Answer me!" shouted the soldier slapping Adalard across the face.

Adalard glanced over to the direction that his sister hid and replied, "No, there is no one else here but my mother, my father and I."

"Very well, you men will do just fine," said the soldier as he and his partner shoved Adalard and his father out the door.

Adelina waited until she heard the soldiers leave and she got out of her hiding place. She saw her mother's lifeless figure on the ground and started to cry. The distraught young girl mumbled something unintelligible and Amber asked, "Brendan, what did she say?"

Brendan was silent for a moment, and then replied, "She said, 'what have I to do now'?"

"It is now time for me to say; bring me back from whence I came," said Andrea, who by now, was in tears too. The scenery changed to its modern scene.

"Well, at least we know what happened now," said Amber, who was obviously upset as well.

Chapter 5

Questions

It was a quiet trip back home but eventually Amber spoke up and asked, "Who started the false legend?"

"I think it was a woman named Carina. She was the daughter of Adelina. From what I heard Adelina died a few years ago. So apparently only Carina can really help us since her sibling is supposedly avoidant of people," said Andrea.

"Yes, but there is only one problem with seeing Carina," said Brendan.

"What??" asked Amber.

"Oh yes, I forgot, Carina lives in Austria," said Andrea embarrassed.

"Well, let's go then!" said Amber getting up out of the boat.

"Amber, are you crazy? It is about three hours by plane and a day at the most by car!" said Brendan.

"Well as the old saying goes; where there's a will, there's a way!" said Amber persistently.

"You never give up, do you?" asked Andrea smiling.

"Nope! Besides, don't you think Germany deserves to know the truth?!" asked the sleuth.

"Yes, but, what can we do? We are just a couple of teenagers," said Brendan.

"Just teenagers? You guys don't realize that just because we're small and not important, doesn't mean we can't get people to listen to what we have to say! We can do so much more too!" exclaimed Amber.

"Oh! Like what?" questioned Andrea who sounded really doubtful.

"You may not believe this, but a little determination, perseverance, and hope can take you a long ways. You just have to believe! Do you honestly want Germany to continue believing this lie or do you want it to believe the truth?" said Amber.

"You make a great argument, Amber. Okay, we will help you. Just tell us what we need to do and we will try to do it!" said Brendan.

"That's what I like to hear!" explained Amber. She thought for a while and then replied,

"We might be able to obtain a round-trip ticket for a plane flight to and from Austria."

"How?" asked Brendan and Andrea in union.

"Brendan, do you have a lot of money saved from your job?" asked Amber.

"Yes, but it would just be enough for me and Andrea.

"That's great! Because I have money left over from baby-sitting, and my job at Camp Mystery! That should get a round-trip ticket!" said Amber excitedly. "I also have money just in case we need it for food, a hotel, or transportation or all!"

"This is all great but we need to get it by our mom and dad," said Brendan becoming sad.

"No worries! Just remember where there's a will..."

"There is a way!" said Andrea and Brendan in unison finishing Amber sentence.

"Right," she replied.

■　■　■　■　■　■　■　■　■　■　■　■　■　■

"Hmmm, I do not know if this is such a good idea, kids," said Uncle Henry.

"I would have to agree," said Aunt Loralee.

"Uncle Henry, Aunt Loralee, we're trying to solve a little mystery and we believe that it is important for us to solve it," explained Amber.

Uncle Henry could see the begging expression in Amber's eye and then replied, "Let me talk with your Aunt."

The two adults went in the living room and the only thing Amber could hear were low whispers. A few minutes later Aunt Loralee and Uncle Henry returned.

Uncle Henry then said, "We have come to a decision... you may go as long as one of us goes with you."

Amber thanked them and the kids went up to their rooms to pack for their next adventure.

■　■　■　■　■　■　■　■　■　■　■　■　■　■

The next day the three teens and Uncle Henry got into the car and headed for the airport. Along the way, Amber was wondering what their next move would be once they arrived in Austria.

The plane ride didn't take that long and once they arrived and got to their hotel the kids raced to their rooms and decided on their next plan of action.

"Let's see if we can look Carina up in the phone book," suggested Amber. The kids looked around, but came up empty.

"Hmmm... do you think anyone would know where she lives?" asked Brendan.

"It's worth a shot," replied Amber.

The trio went to talk to Uncle Henry and told them that they were going to go searching and Uncle Henry replied, "That is fine with me but unfortunately none of you have a cell phone to reach me just in case something bad happens."

Amber thought on this problem for a moment, and then remembered back to her last birthday when she got an orange colored cell phone. Her brother had made it so she could call from anywhere. "Wait a second! I have one with me! It totally slipped my mind!" said Amber excitedly as she whipped out her small cell phone.

"Well then, here is my cell phone number and if you have any problems please call me," replied Uncle Henry writing down his number.

Amber put the number into her cell phone and then the three teens went out of the hotel on their search.

"Amber, do you really think that we will find Carina?" asked Andrea in a doubtful tone.

"Oh, I'm positive. There has got to be some way of tracking her down," said Amber who now was starting to have some doubt as well.

Amber thought long and hard about how they'd find Carina, but then an idea sparked in her mind.

"Maybe we could ask someone where she lives. I mean for all we know she could live a few towns away from here. Also, if her mom was that famous, wouldn't Carina be as well?"

"That is a very good point, Amber, but who will we ask?" asked Andrea.

"Hmmm... good point... well like I said before, if Carina is really well known then probably a lot of people will know where she lives," replied Amber.

"Well, okay, I will go ask that man over there," said Brendan walking over to a newspaper stand.

After a few moments, Brendan came back with a map and said, "Carina lives in the Northern part of this town; she lives up where the old estates are. However, we will have to take a bus to get there; it will take all day if we walk there. And the nearest bus stop is right around the corner."

"This is awesome! Let's go!" exclaimed Amber.

They made it to the bus stop in the nick of time, for the bus was about to leave. Unfortunately the bus was packed with many people. It was so full that the teens had to stand! They were very relieved that their bus stop arrived somewhat quickly and then jumped off and ran to the nearest bench.

"I am glad that ride is over!" exclaimed Andrea.

The other two agreed and then they were off toward the Estates. Once they got in sight of the enormous houses they were awestruck! Each house was of a different color and they all had a very large lawn both in

21

front and in back. Best of all, the houses had a remarkable view of the entire town! "Now, the man said that Carina's house is a light blue color," said Brendan looking around.

"I see it!" exclaimed Andrea pointing to the house farthest away. It was set upon a huge grassy hill. With a lot of huffing and puffing, the group managed to reach the mansion and Brendan knocked on the door. In an instant, a young woman with brown hair and hazel eyes opened the door.

"Are you Carina?" asked Amber.

"No, I am not. I am her servant. May I help you?" asked the girl, drying her hands with a dishtowel.

"We need to ask Carina a few questions," replied Amber.

"What questions would those be?" came an elderly voice behind the servant. "You may come in, I will have my servant serve us tea in the living room."

Chapter 6

The Infiltration

Carina led the teens to her large living room. There was a large stone fireplace and the furniture was made of mahogany and red velvet. There was pretty flower pattern wallpaper that complimented the furniture and there were two large windows with curtains that matched the red velvet. The floors were made up of tile that was almost the same color as the mahogany.

Carina sat down in one of the chairs and the three teens sat down on the large comfy sofa.

"May we ask you a few questions regarding Tear Drop Island?" asked Amber.

"I do not know anything about that island!" said Carina who seemed very nervous.

"Are you sure, ma'am? You are the daughter of Adelina or am I mistaken?" asked Amber who seemed suspicious.

After a moment of silence Amber finally spoke up and said, "Ma'am, we just want to know about the island."

"If you must know about this island, then I will tell you what my mother told me. She told me that someone accidentally started a fire and it engulfed the house and everyone in it. My mother attempted to save her parents and brother but failed and she barely escaped with her life," said Carina in an annoyed tone.

"But that is false!" exclaimed Andrea.

"Excuse me, young lady, but that is not how you speak to an adult. How could you possibly know that it is not true?" questioned Carina in an angry tone.

Andrea looked really embarrassed but Brendan spoke up. "Well, what Andrea is trying to say is that we were curious and happened to go over there and we noticed that the house was still standing," said Brendan.

"Could it not have been someone else's home? Perhaps someone chose to build a house on that island a while after my mother's burnt down," suggested Carina.

"I don't believe that it's anyone's home, the building looks like no one has inhabited it for years including the surrounding area. The only thing it does appear, is that small little animals and birds have been around," said Amber.

"Are you trying to tell me my mother has been lying to me my entire life?" questioned Carina furiously.

"Ma'am, with all due respect, we do believe that she has been lying to you for a reason. It is not a good one but it is a reason nonetheless," said Andrea who finally got over her embarrassment.

"This is an outrage! How dare you call my mother a liar! Get out of my house this instant," shouted the woman getting up from her chair.

Brendan and Andrea quickly got up and headed for the door, but Amber stood her ground and replied, "I am sorry if we've offended you, but we really just want to know. If you feel uncomfortable talking about this I completely understand. We won't disturb you any longer."

As the teens headed out the door, Carina said, "All right, I am willing to listen to you. I can see that you children are not miscreants of any sort."

The three teens turned around and headed back into the living room.

"Ma'am, do you know of anyone who your mother might have talked to?" inquired Amber.

"You may call me Carina if you like. And no, I do not believe my mother mentioned anyone that she confided in..." started Carina, "Oh, but wait one moment, I do believe that my mother had journals. But I cannot think of where they would be for the life of me."

"Carina, don't you have a brother? Maybe your mother gave them to him?" suggested Amber.

Carina looked a little concerned and then replied, "I surely hope they are not with him, if they are, then I will probably never get them."

"Why is that?" asked Brendan.

"Well, my younger brother and I do not get along very well. In fact, we have not talked for quite a while. The last I remember seeing him was at our mother's funeral," replied the elderly woman.

The three teens thought for a moment about how they were going to get those journals. Suddenly a great idea popped into Andrea's mind. "Could we just go to his house and ask him if we may look at the journals?" "Andrea, think about that for a second. I think he'd find it kinda weird if three teens just randomly came up to his door asking him if they could look at his mother's old journals. Not to mention, we're probably the only ones who know about the journals," said Amber.

"Oh, yes, I guess I did not think that completely through," replied Andrea.

"There is only one thing that we must do then... we should sneak into his house," said Brendan.

"I cannot believe I am saying this but, I believe that you are correct, it might be the only way, however, you children must find your own way to his house. I cannot be seen there for he will become suspicious," said Carina.

"How are we supposed to find him then?" asked Amber.

"That is an excellent question, I do not know, he has moved since the funeral and he has not told me where he moved to," replied Carina.

"We'll have to research, that's our only option, but before we can do anything, we need to know his name," said Amber.

"Oh, yes, he is named after our uncle, Adalard. Speaking of names, I neglected to ask you of yours," said Carina, matter of factly.

"Oh yeah, my name is Amber and these are my cousins, Brendan and Andrea."

"Well, Amber, I wish I could have been of more help to you, and I do wish you the best of luck," said Carina as the teens got up to leave.

"Thank you, Carina, and you have been of great help to us," stated Amber.

The teens said their good-byes and then they exited the glorious mansion and went off to find Adalard.

■ ■ ■ ■ ■ ■ ■ ■ ■ ■ ■ ■ ■ ■ ■ ■

"Amber, this is hopeless. We have been looking for where Adalard lives for hours!" exclaimed Andrea who flopped down on the bed in their hotel room.

"Shhhh! Keep it down! Brendan and Uncle Henry are asleep in the other room!" said Amber in a whisper.

"Yes, Amber I do realize this. It is eleven o'clock! And we should get to bed! We can always search tomorrow morning when we are more awake," replied Andrea in a begging manner.

"Maybe your ri... wait! I think I've found something! Oh my gosh! This is it! Wow! All those six hours of researching has finally paid off! See, I told you, Andrea! Andrea?" said Amber looking over at her cousin. But she had finally fallen into a deep sleep.

"Maybe I should follow her lead," whispered Amber too herself. She put her laptop away, got ready for bed and then she fell asleep within a minute.

The next day, after breakfast, Amber got out her computer and copied down Adalard's location. They all got ready and then they caught the crowded bus again and headed toward their destination.

"Phew! Amber, could we please find another way of transportation back to the hotel? I do not think I can take much more of those horrible buses!" exclaimed Andrea, once they got off at their stop.

"I don't know, Andrea, we'll have to see. But let's focus on one thing at a time here," said Amber as she looked down at the direction. "From what these directions say, Adalard lives just a few streets away."

As Amber started walking away the two teens followed after her. And before they knew it they arrived at his house. It was a lot smaller than Carina's house, but yet it was still fairly large. It was a white house with black shutters and it had a few trees in the front but a large, thick forest in the back. The grass was a perfect shade of green and a purple car was clearly seen in front of a small garage.

Amber examined the house for a possible way in. Then she saw that there was an open window on the first floor. "I have an idea," said she to the others, "Brendan and Andrea, I want you to make a diversion, while I go and get the journals."

"How?" questioned Brendan. Amber thought about that for a moment then replied, "Why don't you two go to the door and tell him that you two are writing an article for your school paper and it involves him."

"Okay, we will come up with something like that," said Andrea grinning. They all came up to the house and Brendan knocked on the door while Amber sneaked behind the house. Amber waited until she heard the conversation going.

"Excuse me sir, but we were wondering if you would like to answer a few questions for an article that we are doing!" exclaimed Andrea.

"Why would you like to interview me? I have nothing to say that would interest you," he replied.

"Well, we are technically doing an article on the island your mother once lived on in Germany? Do you know anything of that?" asked Brendan.

"What compelled you to write an article of that tragic story?" he asked.

"We found it interesting and we figured that you were the only one that could give us information," replied Andrea hoping that their cover wouldn't be blown.
"Why did you not go to my know-it-all big sister? I am sure she could help you," said Adalard in a grumpy manner.

Brendan thought quickly and replied, "Why would we go to her? Personally sir, I think you would know a lot more than she would."

Adalard liked this flattery and replied in a smug voice, "I suppose you are right, I know a lot more than she would, you children were very wise to come to me instead of... her. Would you like to come in?"

"Actually, no sir, we would prefer to stay out in the fresh air and we only have a few questions," replied Andrea.

"All right, if you prefer that, then let me hear the first question," said Adalard.

"Wow! They're better actors than I thought!" said Amber to herself as she slid quietly and carefully in through the open window. Once there, she looked around the house to be sure that no one was coming.

Amber scanned the room she was in and realized that the house was much bigger on the inside than the out. "I hope I have enough time to look for the journals before I'm caught!"

Chapter 7

The Truth Is Out

Amber quietly tiptoed around from room to room and came to find nothing of importance until she stumbled upon one green colored room. It was the most elegant room Amber had ever seen, with green drapes and lacy decor and green pattern furniture with a jade carpet! She walked farther in and studied everything. She also noticed the off white wall and examined it thoroughly and her sleuthing soon came to an end, for her eyes fell upon a closet in the corner. She walked over to it and opened the door. Now at first, one would think it was just a plain ordinary closet, but Amber saw that some of the paint on the back wall was starting to peel and it soon revealed a keyhole! "Where is the key?" she wondered to herself. Then she remembered that in one of the rooms, she previously examined, there was an old-fashioned desk.

She went to the other room and rushed over to the desk. She turned over papers and opened drawers. In the last drawer she opened was the key! "Yes, I've got it!" she said to herself.

"You know, breaking and entering is still considered a crime in Austria!" said a voice behind Amber.

Amber swirled around and to her horror saw Carina's brother and her two cousins right beside him.

"We are sorry, Amber! We tried to distract him for as long as we could!" said Andrea who seemed a bit nervous.

"So, what are you doing in my house, Amber?" questioned Carina's brother who seemed more curious than anything.

"Well, um, it's kind of a long story," she replied timidly. "Well, I have got plenty of time," he replied.

Amber realized that there was no escaping now, so she followed him into his living room, which was a smaller version of Carina's living room. All three teens sat on the couch and Carina's brother sat in his big easy chair.

"You children do not seem like the type that would break into some stranger's house for no apparent reason, what are you looking for?" he asked.

Amber spilled the whole story in hopes that Adalard would believe her. When she was through, no one said a word. Then after a few minutes Adalard spoke up, "I am sorry, children, but I find your little story highly unlikely."

"Adalard, sir, to tell you the truth we went and talked to your sister first and the funny thing is, is that she completely believed us," replied Amber.

"What?! You told me that you did not talk to her," exclaimed Adalard.

"Wait! She really told us to talk to you. She said that you could help us," explained Brendan.

"Very well, I suppose that I can help you," said Adalard letting out a big sigh.

"We really appreciate it, sir!" said Amber.

"You are welcome, I will go and retrieve my mother's journals for you. To be honest, I have not even looked through them yet, so you might be right," said Adalard as he was heading up the stairs.

"Here are the journals, they are a bit dusty," announced Adalard entering the living room.

■ ■ ■ ■ ■ ■ ■ ■ ■ ■ ■ ■ ■ ■ ■ ■

The night sky began to appear over the horizon as all three finished reading the journals.

"So did anyone find anything?" asked Amber.

"I did," replied Adalard. "Everything you said is true! My mother was not a hero she was a coward. It was my uncle who saved her!"

"Well, now it is your choice, Adalard. Do you want Germany to finally know the truth or do you want them to continue on believing a lie?" asked Brendan.

"I now believe they should know, they have a right!" he replied.

Amber smiled and said," All right, now that we've established that. How do we let Germany know?"

"There is only one way, but I prefer not to use it." said Adalard.

"Let me guess, your sister?" asked Andrea.

"Yes, she has a job on a radio station as a broadcaster and this radio is heard from all over Austria, Germany and many other surrounding countries!" replied Adalard in a serious voice.

The room went silent, then Andrea spoke up, "She is just a phone call away. Adalard, this also might give you a chance to make amends with your sister."

Adalard started to pick up the phone but then hesitated, "Are you positive that this is the only way the truth can be set free?"

Amber picked up the phone and handed it to Adalard and replied with a slight smile, "It's the only way."

The teens got out of the room and left Adalard to talk to his sister alone. They went out of the house and into the dark moonlit night. While they were outside, Amber picked up her cell phone and called her Uncle. Although he was not happy that they were out so late, he still was happy to hear that their mission was complete and that they were safe.

As soon as the call had ended Adalard came out and had a blank look on his face.

"Are you all right? What did she have to say?" asked Andrea.

"Well, we are on good terms now and she has agreed to spread the word," he replied with a smile," thank you for your help! I will be bringing the journals to her so she may read them as well."

"We are very glad to have helped, Adalard," replied Brendan. As the three teens turned to leave, Adalard called back and said, "If you would like, I could bring you back to your hotel. It is the least I can do!"

Amber looked at her two cousins who had weary looks on their face and she replied, "We would very much appreciate it, thanks!"

The group got into Adalard's car and he drove them back to their hotel. When they exited the vehicle, Adalard said to them, "Thank you again my friends, I will make sure that you get credit for this."

Amber smiled and replied, " Oh, there's no need for that. We're just glad to help."

"I insist! My sister and I cannot take all of the credit! We would have never found out, if you had not come in and opened our eyes to the truth that has been shielded from us our entire lives!" replied Adalard persistently.

"If that is what you wish," replied Brendan in a low tone, for he was carrying his sister who was fast asleep.

At their departure the teens had a restful night's sleep and then in the morning they were on their way back to Germany.

Once they got home the teens unpacked and decided to take a day off from all the exhilarating work that they had done during the past few days.

They got some freshly made chocolate cookies and retired into the living room and turned on the radio. As Brendan flipped through the channels Andrea suddenly said, "STOP!"

Brendan turned back to the previous station to find the news. "What is so interesting about this, Andrea?" asked Brendan who was a bit perplexed.

"Shhhh! Listen!" she exclaimed in a whisper.

Amber wasn't able to comprehend what was being said but lucky for her Andrea translated every word.

"A mystery has been revealed in Germany! Three young sleuths Brendan, Andrea, and their American cousin, Amber, have uncovered a truth that has been hidden from our eyes for many decades! As it turns out, our beloved heroine, Adelina, had not been truthful to us. It was just recently found, in one of her journals, that she did not save her family! Her mother was indeed killed by the Nazis who had invaded the small house, but the Nazi soldiers took the men of the family away. When asked if there were any other members in the house, Adelina's brother, Adalard, said that there were none. He was the one to have saved Adelina. Not the other way around. And, the house is still standing in one piece. I believe I speak for everyone when I say, thank you very much Brendan, Andrea, and Amber!"

"Oh my! We did it!" exclaimed Brendan. Amber sat back in the comfy chair and let out a deep breath, relieved that this difficult mystery was finally solved. The next day was a sad one, for Amber had to depart from her family and the country that she had grown to love. At the airport, many hugs were exchanged and tears followed along.

"We will miss you very much, Amber!" exclaimed Aunt Loralee with tears.

"Same here, Aunt Loralee," replied Amber trying to hold back the tears.

After they exchanged hugs again Amber boarded the plane. Several hours later, the passengers went quiet for it was around midnight. As Amber looked out into the night sky she wondered to herself," What other mystery waits for me back home?"

The End

The Elusive Kidnapper

Chapter 1

A Surprising Appearance

It was a cold, stormy night and Amber Oak was curled up on the windowsill reading a horror novel. The doorbell suddenly rang which made Amber jump a foot in the air. She closed her book and walked down the stairs. "Who could possibly want me or my brother this late at night?" She opened the front door and came face-to-face with some popular kids from school.

"Great, what do you guys want? Don't I get enough of you at school?" she asked with a tone of annoyance.

"Look, Amber, we need your help," said one of the boys whose name was Andrew Meadows.

"I've got better things to do," said Amber closing the door.

Andrew stopped the door and said, "Look, I know you hate Justin and me but we really need your help with a mystery!"

"Why would I ever want to solve a mystery that involved you? Get real!!" replied Amber with anger in her voice.

Both boys were shocked. Amber had never turned down a mystery before. "Please, Amber, just hear us out!" said Justin with a hint of pleading in his voice.

"Okay, you have a few minutes to explain what compelled you to come to my house," said Amber with impatience.

"Alright, my girlfriend, Natalie Park was kidnapped!" explained Andrew.

"Wait, what?! What makes you think that?" asked Amber letting her curiosity show.

"Justin, Natalie, and I were walking downtown. Natalie was behind us and after a few minutes of walking we heard her scream. We turned around to find that Natalie disappeared!" said Andrew.

"Okay, was there an alleyway near where she disappeared?" questioned Amber.

Andrew shook his head no.

"How about a car?" she continued.

"There were a few cars around but nothing seemed out of the ordinary," said Andrew.

"Trust me, we looked everywhere for her!" assured Justin.

"Are you sure she wasn't playing a prank on you?" suggested Amber.

"Actually we considered that and we called her several times but she didn't answer back. We tried back at her house and we asked her mom if she was there and she said no. Now her parents are worried," said Justin.

"Can you think of anyone that would want to kidnap her?" asked Amber.

"Nope, not really," replied Andrew.

"Let me think about this, okay?" said Amber.

"But, Amber, we really need you!" exclaimed Andrew.

"I said, I'll think about it!" she replied, and with that she closed the door.

The next day was a Saturday, which went by slower than normal because she couldn't help but think of this puzzling mystery. Was this a clever prank to embarrass her or was this a genuine mystery? Amber got a glass of water and decided that the best way to get over this was to watch some television. Amber turned it on and flipped through the select few channels that were available...suddenly she came across the news channel whose topic was on Natalie!

"I am here at the scene of the crime, where yesterday, a young woman by the name of Natalie Park disappeared. Sources say that she was walking with her boyfriend Andrew Meadows and her friend Justin Summers. Over to you, John," said the female reporter.

"Thank you, Emily, I am here with the parents of Natalie Park. Mrs. Park, do you have any idea of who took your daughter?" asked John.

"No, she was such a good girl! I can't think of anyone who would do this!" exclaimed Mrs. Park through tears.

"Was there a ransom note?" asked John.

"Yes, there was. It was in a very messy handwriting and I couldn't read it," replied the distraught mother.

Amber turned off the television and realized that this was no prank whatsoever. This was real! Amber looked up Andrew's number and gave him a call.

"Hello? Andrew, I've decided that I'll help you," said Amber.

Chapter 2

The Investigation Begins

Andrew gave Amber directions to his house and Amber headed over there as soon as possible.

"So what convinced you, Amber?" asked Justin.

"The news," she quickly replied.

"So how are we going to find her?" asked Andrew.

Amber was silent for a moment then replied, "I honestly don't know! I can usually follow leads but there aren't any, unless..."

"Unless what?" asked Andrew.

"Follow me!" exclaimed Amber running out the door.

The two guys caught up with Amber and Justin asked, "What's your theory, detective?"

Amber gave Justin a stern look then replied,

"What if there was something that the kidnapper dropped when they snatched Natalie?"

"Good theory, but one problem, the police have searched everywhere!" said Andrew.

"Sometimes the police can overlook things," continued Amber.

The boys gave a shrug and they all walked to the scene of the crime.

"So what are we looking for?" asked Justin.

"Something out of the ordinary," she replied. All three continued to look for quite sometime, that is, until a tiny piece of evidence appeared.

"Hey, look at this! I think I've found something," said Andrew.

Amber looked to where he was pointing and said, "Don't touch it!"

"Why?" asked Justin.

"Because you'll contaminate it!!" she replied as she took out her tweezers.

Amber picked a piece of hair up with the tweezers and asked, "Natalie has blonde hair, right?"

"Yes," replied Andrew.

"Strange, this hair looks red and it looks like it was dyed," said Amber examining it.

"Think it could have come from a dog?" asked Andrew.

"No, it's definitely human, but the fact that it's dyed will make it more difficult to identify who it belongs to," said Amber.

"You know how to tell who a person is just by their hair?" asked Justin.

"Only the FBI could do that," said Amber with a smile, "however, I have a machine at home that can give us a little bit more information on the hair".

"Wow, she really is a freak," whispered Andrew to Justin.

"Hey! You want me to help you, right?" questioned Amber.

"Of course," replied Justin.

"Well, then, quit insulting me," exclaimed Amber with anger in her voice.

The two boys nodded and off they all went to Amber's house.

■ ■ ■ ■ ■ ■ ■ ■ ■ ■ ■ ■ ■ ■ ■ ■

"Okay, Justin, plug this in to the wall socket, and Andrew, flip that yellow switch. We should get the result in about a half-an-hour," said Amber. It took them about an hour to set the machine up.

The teens headed down to the living room and turned the television on.

"How can you watch TV at a time like this?" asked Andrew in shock.

"I'm looking to see if the police have found more info. No need for a panic-attack," said Amber.

"Oh, sorry," replied Andrew feeling embarrassed.

Amber smirked and flipped through the channels to see if she could find any news reports. After a while of searching she came across a news channel, which had Natalie Park as it's prime story.

"I am at the exact spot where young Natalie Park disappeared. Her disappearance is quite a mystery, for this elusive kidnapper has left no clues."

BEEP! BEEP!

"Sorry, forgot to put my cell on vibrate," said Andrew.

"Hello?" said Andrew.

"Andrew it's me, Natalie," said the voice.

"Natalie! Where are you? Are you okay?" questioned Andrew.

Amber and Justin got up from they were sitting and walked over to Andrew.

"I'm fine, Andrew, for now, that is," she replied in a scared voice.

"Where are you?" asked Justin.

"Justin, is that you?" asked Natalie.

"Yes."

"Well honestly, I don't know where I am. All I know is that it's dark and cold," she replied.

"Well, don't worry, honey, Justin and I will find you," said Andrew.

"Excuse me!" said Amber.

"Well, actually Amber Oak is helping us as well, "Andrew added.

"Well, that's great! I'm sure you'll be able to find me with her help! Meanwhile, I'll try to get out," said Natalie.

"Okay, be safe, sweetheart," he replied.

"Oh I... Ahhhhhhhhh," she screamed.

The phone disconnected and the three teens were left standing where they were, speechless.

Chapter 3

The Analysis

"What are we going to do?" asked Justin.

"The analysis should be done now, let's go check it out," said Amber.

The three teens headed upstairs and went to the machine. Amber did a few things on her computer and came to a solution.

"This is definitely human hair, and the machine revealed the type of dye, however it doesn't indicate where it's sold," explained Amber.

"Well, how long do you think it'll take you to find out?" asked Andrew.

"I don't really know. I've never done this type of analysis before. Maybe a day at the most," said Amber.

"Amber, Natalie may not have a day!" exclaimed Andrew.

"I do realize this, and I'll call you when I figure it out," said Amber sympathetically.

The two boys, although upset by Amber's news, understood and went back home for it was quite late.

■　■　■　■　■　■　■　■　■　■　■　■　■

"Hello?" said Andrew in a groggy voice.

"Hey Andrew, it's Amber. I've go something."

Andrew looked at his clock, which read 3:00 am and figured that Amber would not have called unless it was really important, "All right, let me call Justin." He called Justin, who was more annoyed by the early phone call, but said he'd be at Amber's house shortly. Amber opened the front door as soon as she heard the doorbell ring.

"Okay, Amber, this better be important enough for you to call me at three a.m.," said Andrew.

"Well, actually, it is. Follow me," she replied.

"Wait, your brother doesn't mind us coming here at like five in the morning?" asked Justin.

"I told him the circumstances and he has always been supportive of my investigations so he was cool with it," replied Amber walking up the stairs.

When they got to her room the boys noticed that it was much messier then the day before. "She must really be into her work!" thought Andrew to himself.

"I found out this dye is sold at many salons," said Amber.

"So that's the great news? We woke up at three in the morning for this?" exclaimed Justin in frustration.

"Look, I'm sorry! I thought if we put our brains together we would think of something. I'll keep searching. You guys go back home and get some sleep," said Amber, who was very discouraged now.

"Thank you!" said Justin, turning to leave.

"Justin, wait. We asked Amber to help us with this mystery. It's our mystery and I think it's unfair if we have her do all the work. We'll stay and help," said Andrew.

"You will?!" exclaimed Amber with a smile appearing on her face.

"We will?" asked Justin who was hoping to sleep a bit longer.

"Yes, we will! How can we help?"

Amber thought for a moment then replied, "We can start a search online for any salons near here that sell it."

"That's a really good idea...but first...you got any coffee?" asked Justin.

"Justin, don't be so rude!" exclaimed Andrew.

Amber couldn't help but laugh. Who would have thought that these popular kids would be kind towards her! "I'll go make some! Why don't you come down and help me?" suggested Amber.

A small smile formed on Andrew's face as he replied, "Something tells me you don't trust us alone with your computer."

"No! Really?! What gave you that idea?" asked Amber sarcastically.

"We're trying to be as cooperative and nice as possible," said Justin defensively.

Amber stopped in the doorway, turned around and replied, "Did it ever occur to you that that doesn't matter to me?"

"I don't understand," said Andrew, who was very confused.

"Of course you wouldn't, it's all a matter of trust. Even though we're working together on this case, it doesn't mean I trust you any more than I did last week," stated the frustrated detective.

The two boys stood there in silence, both thinking similar thoughts. They never had to think that their actions spoke louder than their words!

Amber then made her way down the stairs and the boys followed slowly after in silence, afraid they'd hit another nerve.

■　■　■　■　■　■　■　■　■　■　■　■　■　■　■

Coffee was later served and the trio made their way back to Amber's room. The awkward silence eventually left and they were all back to discussing the case.

"Have you found anything, Amber?" asked Andrew.

"Actually, I might have! The only place that sells this dye that is near here is at a hair salon downtown."

"Well, let's go then," said Justin taking a sip of his coffee.

"Can't do that yet, the place doesn't open till ten," replied Amber.

"What do we do till then?" asked Andrew.

"Chris will be awake soon, maybe he can make us breakfast," said Amber.

A little while later Chris was up and Amber raced downstairs to explain to him what was going on, "Really, Amber? Waking people up that early isn't very nice."

"What can I say, I was really excited!" she replied.

Chris smiled and replied, "How do pancakes for breakfast sound?"

Amber nodded and ran upstairs to tell the guys. To her dismay she found them with a look of horror spread across their faces, "What happened?"

Andrew silently handed her his cell phone and she saw a text message from Natalie, "This is odd, one would think the kidnapper would take her cell phone away after she called," thought Amber to herself. However, this message was not from Natalie, it was from the kidnapper! It said:

"She is mine and none can have her!! Give up now while you still can, or your precious Natalie will be dead."

"That's original. Well, the last part is, I am having a hard time wrapping my head around the 'she is mine and none can have her' part...that is different. Typically kidnappers request money for their victims," said Amber pacing the room.

The two guys were silent and distraught. They couldn't figure out how to handle the situation. This was their first mystery and it involved someone they cared about.

"Come on guys, let's go downstairs, Chris may have breakfast done," said Amber heading out the door. Justin and Andrew slowly rose from where they sat. "I'm not sure if I'm hungry anymore," said Andrew. Justin agreed. "Well, we are no use to Natalie if we're all starving," stated Amber.

"No, I guess not," said Andrew.

They followed Amber downstairs and into the kitchen. Amber finished much quicker than the guys and raced upstairs to get changed. As they ate, the guys just pushed their food around their plate...how in the world could they eat at a time like this?

Chris noticed this and sat down at the table, "Don't worry guys, Amber is the best person for a job like this! Did you know she helped regain Germany's lost memory?"

"Huh?" asked Justin and Andrew in union.

"Wow, you guys are so not in the loop! Yeah! She totally solved like the largest mystery over in Germany that changed the course of history. If she can do that...then I am more than positive she can find your girlfriend, Andrew," replied Chris.

"If you're certain and if she does solve this mystery. I would be forever in her debt," replied Andrew.

"Ditto," said Justin.

"That's nice of you, you know it's just her and me, and even though we look like a happy family, truth is, we struggle," explained Chris in a melancholy tone.

"We're really sorry," said Andrew.

"Tell that to her," replied Chris.

A few moments later Amber came racing down the stairs and said, "You guys ready to go? It's close to ten."

"Yep! Let's hurry!" said Justin.

"Good luck, guys!" yelled Chris as all three ran out the door and to Justin's car.

■ ■ ■ ■ ■ ■ ■ ■ ■ ■ ■ ■ ■ ■ ■

"So where is this place exactly?" asked Justin once they got into town.

"Okay, do you know where Bridge Street is?" asked Amber. Justin nodded.

"Well, the number of the building is number 192 and it's down that road," she continued.

Justin understood and started driving downtown. While they were in the car Andrew asked, "Amber, where the heck did you get a machine that could tell so much?"

"I made it. I like to invent things that help me with my investigations. That hair analyzer machine is a new invention," she replied.

"Wow, it's actually pretty cool that you're smart enough to build complex inventions like that," said Justin.

"Well, Amber, I must say you're a lot different than I expected and much smarter," said Andrew.

"You'll find that I'm much different then the every day teenage girl. While all the other girls my age shop and fuss over their make-up, I'd rather just sit home curled up on the windowsill reading a book or inventing something new," the detective replied.

Amber looked at Andrew's expression and she could have sworn she saw a smile sweep across his face, or was it the sun playing tricks on her eyes? No, she was definitely sure it was a smile.

They finally reached their destination and all three went inside what appeared to be a very expensive salon.

"Excuse me, Ma'am," said Amber to the lady at the front desk, "Do you still carry this brand of hair dye?"

Amber got out a piece of paper with a French title on it and gave it to the stylist.

"Well, as a matter of fact I do!" replied the lady.

She disappeared into the stock room and returned in a few minutes. "I have only a few in stock," she replied.

"Can you please give me the list of people who have bought this product in the past week?" asked Amber.

The lady gave Amber a curious look and replied, "Why would you want that?"

Amber thought of the first excuse that came to her mind, "We are working with the police on a case, the kidnapping of Natalie Park. They found some evidence that led to your store. They asked us to request a list of the most recent purchases, of that particular dye."

The hairdresser looked at each teen suspiciously then replied, "How do I know you're not lying to me?"

"Well, I can always call my boss, Officer Shelton, and I can explain to him that you are not cooperating with us. Now, if I'm not mistaken, this could mean a lot of trouble for you and…" said Amber.

"Okay, okay, I get your point! I don't feel like losing my job. I'll print you out a copy," interrupted the nervous woman.

"Thank you for your cooperation ma'am, the police department will be very happy," said Amber taking the piece of paper and heading out the door.

Once they were outside, and out of hearing range, the boys looked at Amber in shock.

"You should see the look on your faces right now!" laughed Amber.

"I can't believe you did that, I didn't know you could lie like that!" exclaimed Justin.

"Well, it wasn't a total lie, I do know Officer Shelton down at the station," said Amber innocently, "anyway, let's get down to business. Do either of you know the names on the list?"

Andrew looked over the paper with Justin reading over his shoulder.

"Haven't heard of these people," said Justin.

"Me neither, but maybe Mrs. Park has," said Andrew in a hopeful tone.

"Only one way to find out..." replied Amber heading to the car.

Chapter 4

The Mystery Deepens

DING, DONG!

Footsteps were heard coming towards the door, and the same woman on the television opened the door.

"Hello Andrew! Who are your friends?" greeted Mrs. Park.

"Hello Mrs. Park, I'm Amber Oak, your daughter's boyfriend asked me to help solve the mysterious kidnapping of your daughter."

The woman's face started to glow and her eyes grew big and she replied, "Oh my goodness! You're the detective Amber Oak! I've heard so much about your cases. My daughter's a huge fan of yours! I'm so relieved you're here, you'd probably do a much better job than any professional detective."

Amber smiled at the woman's reaction and replied,

"I do have some good news for you and I also think you could help us in this investigation."

"Oh, I'd love to help you," she replied.

The woman let them in and led them to the living room. She gestured for them to sit down and Amber spilled everything including the phone call and the text message

"So, my baby girl is still out there?" asked the woman.

Amber nodded, "Mrs. Park, I was wondering if I could look at that ransom letter?"

"We only have a copy of it. The police took the original, but you may see it," replied the woman handing the copy to Amber.

Amber examined the letter very carefully, "I know what it says but it doesn't really make much sense."

"Well, what does it say, Amber?" asked Justin.

"It says, that he either gets money for what the girl is worth, by sundown at the old graveyard, or Natalie is his forever.

"Mrs. Park, could you take a look at this list and see if anyone on it rings a bell?" asked Andrew.

"Well, let's see, I only know of one of these people on the list, it's Henry Matthews. He was Natalie's ex-boyfriend," replied Mrs. Park.

"WHAT??!!" questioned the boys in union.

"I told you it didn't make any sense!" said Amber. "Mrs. Park, why do you think he'd write this?"

A pale look swept across Mrs. Park's face and she replied, "He and Natalie were so close, well, that is, until Henry was getting to overprotective of Natalie. He wouldn't let her out of his sight! It was so pathetic; it was as if Natalie was his life!! He would go everywhere with her! I tried to tell Natalie that he isn't the right guy for her, but she wouldn't listen to me. Eventually she found out the hard way. She was at one point talking to one of her best friends, Michael. Henry saw them talking and he immediately thought that Michael was flirting with Natalie, so he attacked Michael.

Andrew was astonished and replied, "Natalie never told me about that!"

"She probably didn't want you to be upset or for that matter put you in danger," said Mrs. Park.

"Do you really think that Henry would kidnap Natalie?" asked Justin.

"Well, of course, he has the perfect motive!" she replied.

"Where does he live?" asked Amber.

"He was never clear on where he lived," said Mrs. Park.

"Well, then, we'll just find out," said Amber getting up to leave.

"How are we going to do that?" asked Andrew.

"It's called the internet, now come on! Thank you for your time, Mrs. Park," replied Amber.

The other two followed Amber out the door and to the car. Amber told Justin to drive back to her house. As soon as they parked in the driveway Amber jumped out and headed to the door. She got inside and ran to the computer.

"Amber, what are you looking for?" asked Justin.

"I'm looking to see where Henry Matthews lives," she replied.

The guys decided not to question her any farther.

"It doesn't say much, just that he won a few awards as a kid in elementary school," said Amber.

"Great, just what we need, a dead end," said Justin in despair.

Amber stared intently at the computer screen for some time, as if she was deep in thought. Then an idea sparked, "I have a few ideas but I'm not sure how well they would work."

"Care to share, detective?" asked Andrew.

Amber picked up the phone, dialed a number and motioned for the guys to be quiet.

"Yes, I would like to speak to Officer Shelton...this concerns a kidnapping," said Amber.

Amber put the phone on speaker and just as she did, a voice came over and said, "Whom am I speaking with?"

"Hello, Officer, its Amber Oak."

"Why, hello, Amber! I haven't heard from you in quite a while! How have you been? What can I do for you?"

"Well, you could help me out with a case I am working on. It involves a kidnapping and I may have a potential kidnapper. I just need to get more information on him and his potential whereabouts," she replied professionally.

"I can see what I can do, Amber, but you must remember that many of the people on file here or anywhere for that matter have confidential things. But I will see what I can look up real quick. What is your criminal's name?"

"Henry Mathews."

"Okay, let's see what I can pull up here on the computer."

"Hmmm, that's interesting."

"What?" asked Amber.

"Well it says here that Mr. Mathews has many accounts and accusations against him."

"What are these accounts and accusations?"

"Amber, what does this have to do with finding where he lives?" whispered Justin.

Amber covered the mouthpiece and replied, "The more information we get on Mathews, and the more we have against him in court once we catch him. Plus it's safer for us to see if he really is our guy."

"Amber, are you still there?" asked the Officer.

"Yes, I am. So what do you have?"

"There is stalking, petty theft, death threats, many of these are considered minor, but if you can catch him involved with kidnapping we may be able to put him away for a few years."

"Thank you very much, sir, where does he live?"

"I'm not sure how that would help you, Amber. I highly doubt he would keep his captive at his own home. But he lives on the north side of the town, the countryside. It's 122 Pine Road. I hope this helps and if you need my help I am just a call away," said the Officer.

"Thank you very much for your help, Officer Shelton. By the way, this kidnapping is the one involving Natalie Park. Her boyfriend and other friend have asked me to help solve the case. They are with me as we speak. We have been searching for two days now. We have received a threat through the boyfriend's cell phone from the kidnapper. We also had a lead from Natalie's mother. She told us of Mathews because we found a piece of bright red hair at the crime scene which we found out to be a special dye that is only sold at a local hair salon downtown. Mathews is only connected to Natalie because they had dated a while back, now during their relationship he was obsessed with her and became jealous whenever she talked to other guys. The threat and the ransom note we received had the same idea in a sense, they both stated that 'Natalie would be his' or along those lines," said Amber.

Silence...

"Well, that certainly is a lot to take in, I will talk to the other officers here and we will be ready to take action. Would you like us to check his place out, Amber? After all, it seems like you've got this case pretty well under control."

"Actually sir, with all due respect, I think it'd be best if me, Natalie's boyfriend, and friend searched. We might be able to detect something you and your men may not. Not to mention, if Mathews is at his house he could be scared off by the sirens."

"I understand this, but Amber, you're dealing with a kidnapper who may be potentially armed. Are you positive you can do this?" asked the Officer with a hint of concern in his voice.

"I'm more than positive. Many underestimate me and come to find out that I'm perfectly capable of handling myself, I have my trusty pocketknife, and this kidnapper doesn't seem that smart. He seems quite the amateur, if you ask me."

"All right, Amber, but I will have my people standing by the phones if you need back up, good luck!"

"Thank you, Officer Shelton!"

"So you guys ready to go?" asked Amber as she hung up the phone.

"I am, but you sounded like a real detective there for a minute!" exclaimed Andrew.

"You sound surprised, you have to know how to work with people in order to get what you need, that includes talking the way they talk," explained Amber.

"Well, what are we waiting for, let's go catch a kidnapper!" said Justin.

■ ■ ■ ■ ■ ■ ■ ■ ■ ■ ■ ■ ■ ■ ■ ■

They traversed around the countryside for quite some time, until they came to a cluster of small houses.

"This is the house," said Amber pointing to one house on the hill.

"Doesn't look like anyone's home," said Justin.

"Okay, Justin, park a little ways in the woods," said Amber.

"Why?" he questioned.

"We're gonna investigate the house and I don't want the car to be seen. I do want it to be close to the house just in case we need to get a quick getaway," said Amber.

"So we're gonna break in?! Amber, don't you think that's carrying it a bit too far?" asked Andrew nervously.

"Andrew, you have to understand, this is an emergency. Natalie could be in serious trouble if not worse! Trust me, I don't break into houses often," she replied.

"Wait, so you've done this before?!" asked Justin in a shocking tone.

"Well, yes but only once. I was solving a mystery over in Germany and it sort of led into a bigger mystery," she replied, "Enough chatting, let's get to investigating."

The other two agreed and then quietly set off for the house.

Chapter 5

A Close Call

Amber and the two boys walked closer to the house and they instantly noticed the beauty of it. It was a log house, with a large, well-kept yard.

"This place doesn't look like it would be the home of a delusional type kidnapper," said Justin.

"Rule number one of being a detective, you must always remember, appearances are deceiving," said Amber in a half whisper.

With that, the teens walked to the front door.

"Great, it's locked!" exclaimed Andrew.

"Not a problem, I've got a lock pick," said Amber getting her gadget out.

"Do you have everything?" questioned Justin with a slight smile.

"Uh, nope, I don't have a car. Hoping to get one soon, though," she replied.

Amber finally got the door unlocked and they entered the house. The inside of the house had a beautiful old antique style.

"Okay let's try to find Henry's room. We might find some clues there," suggested Amber.

The others agreed and they searched the house. After a while, a call was heard from the upstairs.

"Amber, Justin, get up here, I've found Henry's room!"

Amber and Justin rushed up the stairs and found Andrew in Henry's room. The room wasn't like the rest of the house. It had posters all over the walls, a computer, and TV. Well, pretty much what one would find in a teenage boy's room. Amber took notice of the computer and went over and turned it on.

"Amber, what are you doing?" asked Justin.

"I'm trying to see if Henry emailed Natalie in the past few weeks," she replied.

"How can you figure that out, without a username and password?" asked Andrew, who again was very confused.

"It's called hacking," said Amber.

"Amber, I'm confused, are you a detective or are you a spy?" asked Justin.

"I just happen to know how to get myself out of certain situations and sometimes they're risky. See, I only use my full knowledge of being a detective when it's an emergency," she replied, "Okay, I'm in his email, now let's see who he's been writing to. Wow! He has written to Natalie! Here's what one email says:

Hey Nat,

I really miss you, I'm sorry for what I did to you! I was a jerk, but I really do love you!

Love, Henry

"That sounds sincere enough," said Justin.

"Yeah but take a look at her response," said Andrew.

Henry,

I don't love you anymore! You really hurt me and I don't want to repeat what has happened!

Natalie

"The other emails are similar," said Amber.

"Not this one!" said Justin, taking over the mouse, "it's from Henry and it sounds pretty threatening."

Natalie,

You are a lovely girl you will want me soon. You will love me; I'll do whatever is necessary to get you to love me. I know who your new boyfriend is and if you don't break up with him, I'll make your life miserable. Trust me when I say this, I'm going to get you no matter what the cost is!

    Henry

    "It looks like Natalie never responded to the email. Henry also emailed this letter to Natalie the night before she vanished!" exclaimed Andrew with worry.

    Amber printed the emails out and Justin asked, "Why are you printing them out?"

    "It's for evidence," replied Amber.

    Suddenly the sound of a car door came from the driveway. Amber, who now was in stealth mode, slowly made her way to the window and saw someone who appeared to be Henry!

    "We gotta get out of here!" she exclaimed in a whisper. As soon as the guys realized what was causing Amber to panic they were already on their way out the door. They all made their way down the stairs and stopped dead in their tracks, for the doorknob on the front door started to turn. Amber thought quickly and noticed a back door. She grabbed Andrew and Justin's wrists and pulled them toward the back door. They all got out just in the nick of time. The villain had just entered the house. Amber slowly got up from her hiding spot and peeked in the window. Suddenly, the villain's face shot up in front of her!

    "RUN!!!" yelled Amber.

    The guys didn't hesitate at all. They ran off to the woods where the car was parked. They jumped in and drove off.

    "Wow, that was close! Now what do we do? Henry knows we are on his case!" exclaimed Justin.

"I have an idea, drive downtown to the scene of the crime," said Amber.

Justin did as she said and before they knew it they were there.

"What are you looking for now, Amber?" asked Andrew in an annoyed tone.

"You said that when Natalie disappeared, nothing was around at the time except an alleyway and a sewer, right?" asked Amber.

Andrew nodded and said,

"Yeah but, we searched the alleyway and nothing was there! Even the police did!"

"Try thinking outside the box, if Henry is as smart as I think he is, he probably wouldn't hide her in a place that the police could find," said Amber.

"Well, where would you suggest, Miss Detective?" asked Justin.

"I'd suggest the sewer, there are a lot of tunnels down there. Who knows, there could even be a secret room," replied Amber.

"I think you've been reading way too many detective novels, Amber," said Andrew.

"That may be true, but I want to check it out! Now, all I need is a flashlight and a pry bar," said Amber.

Justin went to the trunk of his car and said, "I don't have a pry bar but I have a jack handle."

"That will do, just give me a flashlight too."

Justin walked over to Amber and handed her the tools. She sat down on the road and pried at the black, greasy, cover. She asked for the boy's help and with great difficulty the cover was lifted. She took the flashlight and looked down the sewer.

"What do you see, Amber?" asked Justin.

"Well, I was right about the tunnels. Come on, let's go check it out!" said Amber.

The other two were reluctant but they ended up going with her.

"Ugh! It smells down here!" exclaimed Andrew.

"Hello! It's a sewer!" said Amber.

The teens walked further on and found several tunnels.

"Which one do we go down?" asked Andrew.

"Good question," said Amber, "How about we each go down a tunnel and see if we find anything."

"Sure, but how will we be able to contact each other?" asked Andrew.

"Well, um… before we went down in the sewer, I grabbed three walkie-talkies out of my car," said Justin.

Amber was astonished and replied, "That's very good thinking there, Justin."

Justin smiled and each set off for their tunnel.

Chapter 6

The Kidnapper

Amber searched the tunnel thoroughly but she still couldn't find anything. She got to thinking that this was the wrong tunnel, that is, until something shimmering caught her eye. It appeared to be a silver locket in the shape of a heart. Amber picked it up and opened it. Inside was a tiny picture of Andrew and a girl that Amber assumed to be Natalie. She examined her other surroundings and found one set of footprints and a set of drag marks coming from another tunnel near by. "So that's how he got in," thought Amber to herself. She reached for her walkie-talkie and summoned the guys.

"Hey, I've found something!" she exclaimed. Within fifteen minutes the other two reached to where Amber was.

"Amber, what did you find?" asked Justin.

"It's Natalie's locket!" she replied. Andrew took it from her and examined it. His face turned deathly pale and he said,

"Blood, there's some blood on here! Henry's hurt her!"

"Don't worry, Andrew, he's not gonna get away with this," said Amber in her most comforting tone.

"Yeah, it's not over, not by a long shot!" said Justin who seemed a little disturbed by the blood. All three managed to pull themselves together and they continued to walk down the tunnel, which seemed to go on forever. Finally, after about an hour they reached the end.

"Are you kidding me?" said Andrew who was outraged.

The tunnel did end, but it was a dead end.

"There is something here, I just know it. Andrew, Justin search for something out of the ordinary," said Amber.

The boys weren't going to try to argue anymore. They already figured out that Amber knew a lot more about what was going on then they. So they did as she said. Suddenly Justin came across something.

"Hey guys, I've found something," he said. They came over to Justin and looked to where he pointed. It looked to be an outline of a small door.

"This must be where Henry took Natalie!" exclaimed Amber.

Amber got out her dark green pocketknife and tried to pry the door open. When she got a hold of the door, the other two helped her pull it open. They got it but with great difficulty. Amber turned on the flashlight and she started going down the tunnel with the boys right behind her. They all knew within a minute that they were close to finding Natalie for they heard muffled cries.

Once at the end of the tunnel they came upon a startling sight. Natalie was gagged and both her hands and feet were tied. Fortunately Henry was not in sight, but that got Amber worried. He could show up any second with a surprise attack!

"Natalie!" cried Andrew. He rushed over to her and gently took the gag off while Justin used his own pocketknife to cut the bindings.

"Natalie, are you okay?" asked Amber.

"Sort of. When Henry took me I cut my hand on something sharp," she replied holding her badly bandage hand up.

Justin looked at it and replied, "It looks infected, but other than that, how are you feeling?"

"Not so good, I think the infection got to me," she said.

Amber put her wrist on Natalie's forehead and said, "She has a pretty bad fever."

"I wonder when that psychotic ex-boyfriend of yours will show up," asked Justin.

"Oh, I'm already here," replied a cold, menacing voice behind them.

The three teens spun around and looked into the malicious face of Henry Matthews!

"You'll never get away with this!" exclaimed Justin.

"Well, I kinda already have considering I've got the most famous young sleuth around, trapped along with her wanna-be-detective friends!" said Henry with a chilling laugh.

"Well, if I'm so well known, then you must know a lot about me," said Amber.

"Oh yes, I've heard of every single case you've been on. I know you've time-traveled, met up with ghosts, and solved mysteries that were much older than you," he replied.

"I'm impressed, I have a stalker now!" said Amber.

"I don't think stalker is the correct word, I just merely like to find out who I am dealing with, just as you like to find out who you're dealing with," explained Henry.

"Henry, I don't think you realize how serious this is. You can go to jail for kidnapping Natalie and I'm more than positive her parents would have no problem pressing charges," said Amber.

"That's not gonna happen! Natalie is mine! She will always be mine! You, Miss Detective, stuck your nose in a situation where it doesn't belong! She loves me! She wants to be with me!" screamed Henry.

"Henry! Look at her, will you?! Does she look happy or healthy for that matter?" exclaimed Amber.

Henry looked over to Natalie curled up in a ball against Andrew. That got him more furious than ever. "HEY, GET AWAY FROM HER!"

Henry advanced towards Andrew in a threatening manner. He raised his fist ready to strike, but Amber intercepted it. She shoved him out of the way knowing Henry's rage would immediately turn towards her. That moment Natalie, Andrew, and Justin saw a side of Amber that not many get the chance to witness; she was fighting for their lives! The kidnapper was growing weak because of his wild swings and Amber's strong strikes. Suddenly he collapsed. Amber had won.

"Come on, guys, get Natalie out of here, he'll be out for a while," commanded Amber.

"What about you?" asked Andrew picking the half conscious girl up.

"I'm staying here to make sure he doesn't get up. Just to let you know there are cops out there surrounding the crime scene now," said Amber, keeping her eye on the fallen kidnapper.

"Wait, how do you know that?" asked Justin.

"I'll explain later, just hurry and get her out of here, she doesn't look like she has much time left."

The guys left in a hurry and Henry slowly woke up, but he was to weak to get to his feet. He looked up at Amber with a malicious expression, "If you know what was good for you, you'd stay right where you are," warned the young detective.

Not a moment too soon, Officer Shelton, Justin, and Andrew came through the door, "Great work, Miss. Oak. I'm not going to even ask how you solved this case. But, rest assured, he'll be behind bars for quite some time!" The Officer read Henry his rights and led him out the door.

"So Amber, how did the police get here so fast?" asked Andrew.

"Well, I have a pager which instantly connects me to the police and when I heard a cry I pressed the button, summoning Officer Shelton, who knew that meant I found Natalie. He had men ready to go anyway, so that's how they got here so fast."

"Very clever!" exclaimed Justin.

"Thanks, I assume Natalie is on her way to the hospital?"

"Yeah, her mom is in the ambulance with her, she was so relieved to see her," said Andrew, as they got closer to the end of the tunnels.

"I'd imagine any mother would!" replied Amber.

They got out of the sewer and found many cameras aimed at them, Amber thought to herself, "Great, just what I need, people asking me questions... where's Chris when I need him?"

As if he read her mind, Chris came driving up in his old Volkswagen, "Hey kiddo, thought you could use some backup! Hop in!"

"See you guys later!" said Amber to the guys. She hopped into the car and Chris asked, "Where to now?"

"Home, I'm so tired! I haven't slept in two days."

"Sounds good to me," he replied stepping on the accelerator.

A week past and Amber was yet again curled up on the windowsill reading a horror novel. The doorbell rang and Amber ran down the stairs and answered it. Right in the doorway stood Andrew and Justin.

"Hey, Amber, we just wanna say thanks and we'll do anything to pay you back," said Justin.

"Anything?" questioned Amber in shock.

"Anything within reason," replied Andrew with a smile.

"Okay, I'd love it if you can make sure your friends would stop making fun of me and make them stop harassing me!" said Amber seriously.

"That's partially our fault. We started it, but that's because we didn't really know you then," said Justin.

"That still doesn't give you a right to make fun of someone just because you don't know them!" said Amber.

"We know, and we're extremely sorry for that. We'll definitely make sure that that is changed," said Andrew.

Amber smiled and then asked, "How's Natalie?"

"Why don't you ask her yourself?" asked Justin.

Natalie appeared behind the two boys and gave Amber a huge hug.

"Thank you so much Amber, you saved me from that psycho! I too, am in your debt," said Natalie with a smile.

"Just tell me when and where the next mystery will be," said Amber with a little laugh.

The others laughed as well. After a while, they left and Amber went back to her reading. As she was walking back a warm feeling overcame her. She finally realized that people can change and she also made some new friends.

The End

The Legend of the Silver Chest

Chapter 1

A Strange Letter

Amber Oak was sitting in the comfort of her living room working on her homework when the mailman arrived. She laid her pen down, set her homework aside and went to retrieve the mail. When she reached the mailbox, she stopped, looked around and took a deep breath. She noticed the sun reflecting off of the trees and she could hear some birds singing off in the distance. "What a nice day," she thought. As she flipped through the bills, junk mail and fliers, she suddenly came across a light blue envelope addressed to her. She brought the mail in and set it on the kitchen table, picked the blue envelope out of the pile, then sat down and opened it.

It said:

Dear Amber Oak,

My name is Renalia. I am from Galacia and I need your help. I cannot explain what the issue is, for I am afraid this message might be intercepted somehow. Please come to Galacia. If you are able to come, please meet me in front of the Queen's Palace at twelve pm. sharp on Saturday, November 14th.

Regards,

Renalia

As she re-read the letter, she became rather curious. "How does this girl know who I am," she thought, "and how does she know my address? Something tells me today is going to be more than just nice." After studying the letter for a few minutes, Amber decided to talk to her brother Chris to see if she could get the okay from him to go to Galacia.

■ ■ ■ ■ ■ ■ ■ ■ ■ ■ ■ ■ ■ ■ ■

"Absolutely not, Amber!" exclaimed Chris.

"Why not?" questioned Amber.

"Because your adventures are becoming too dangerous now! Remember last time? You were dealing with a kidnapper! Did you really think this mystery through? You don't even know the girl, do you?" replied Chris.

"No, but that's beside the point. What if this girl really is in trouble?" asked Amber.

"I don't want to discuss this any further, you're not going and that's final!!" said Chris in a stern voice.

Amber was very angry. She stormed upstairs to her room and sat on her bed. She thought her brother was being unfair. She had always wanted to go to Galacia because she had heard so much about it. She remembered that Galacia was a rural country and that it was north of the United Kingdom. It was a large island, and she also remembered that it was best known for its roses. As Amber was imagining Galacia she heard a knock on her door.

"Amber, are you in there?"

Silence.

"Amber, look, I'm sorry I got you mad."

She tried to think of something mean to say.

"Amber, please talk to me! I'm really sorry!"

"Go away!" was all she could conjure up.

"Amber, I've decided you can go," he replied.

"I said GO AWAY!" she yelled. "Wait, huh?"

Amber got up from the bed and opened the door. She gave him a huge hug and a peck on the cheek and said, "Thank you, thank you, thank you!"

"Wait a minute," she said, eyeing him suspiciously, "what made you change your mind?"

"Well, I called up a friend of mine over in Galacia and I asked him if he wouldn't mind watching you for about three weeks," replied Chris.

Amber started packing instantly. She was so excited that she didn't even mind that her brother had found her a babysitter.

. . . .

"Amber, are you sure Renalia said she was going to be here?" asked Roger. Roger was a long time friend of Chris. They had met in college. Normally Roger would be patient, but he had been waiting around with Amber for quite some time.

"I'm positive," she replied, sounding just a little frazzled. It had been a long plane flight and she was so anxious to meet this girl that she had Roger drive her to the meeting point right from the airport. They had been waiting for well over an hour now and Amber was getting irritated. "Let's wait just a little longer." Just as she spoke, a young girl with light brown hair wearing a black hooded jacket with blue jeans came running out of a side street toward them.

"Hello, are you Amber Oak?" asked the girl in between breaths.

Amber nodded.

"Hello, I am Renalia," she replied, "I am so glad you could come!"

"Yes, it took a bit of convincing on my part," said Amber with a smile.

"Oh?" said Renalia, with a suspicious look at Roger.

"Oh, not him, this is Roger, my brother's friend, I'm staying at his house while I'm in Galacia. Sort of like a temporary big brother." explained Amber.

"Oh!" said Renalia with a look of understanding, "Is he trustworthy?"

"I assume so, I don't know him very well, but my brother seems to think he is," replied the sleuth.

"Well, just to be cautious, may we talk in private?" asked Renalia.

"Sure, we can go back to Roger's house," suggested Amber.

"I would like that," replied Renalia.

They all got into the car and Roger drove them back to his house. When they arrived Amber got out of the car, stretched, and looked around. Most of the buildings looked to be falling apart and those that weren't, were all boarded up. It smelled of rotting garbage, musty old buildings, and sewage. She could see a stray cat darting from one ally to the next and a dog was heard howling from the distance. "What a difference it is here from the rest of Galacia!" thought Amber. She got her stuff out of the trunk and they went into the house. Roger directed the girls to Amber's room. "Go up the stairs and turn left. The bathroom is at the end of the hall." The girls went up to the room and Amber started unpacking with Renalia's help. As soon as they were done they both sat down and Amber started speaking,

"So how did you find out about me?"

Renalia smiled a bit and replied, "A friend of mine told me about your incredible capabilities of solving mysteries. You might know him. His name is Adalard."

Amber thought back to her past mysteries and recalled the case where she helped Germany regain a lost memory.

"Yes, I know him," replied Amber with a smile.

"Well, I need your help, Amber," replied Renalia. "I think something is wrong. My parents have been acting quite strange lately."

"What do you mean?" asked Amber.

"Well, when I ask them about my heritage and past they always clam up. It is like they do not want to talk to me about it," she replied.

"That is strange. I wonder why they would try to hide your past?" questioned Amber.

"That is what I want you to help me figure out. Not only that, but they have been very distant from me lately," continued Renalia.

"What if we looked you up on the computer?" suggested Amber.

"Excuse me? How could you do that?" asked Renalia.

"You can find out just about anything about anyone on the Internet." explained Amber, "Let's go ask Roger if he has a laptop or a computer that we can use."

They went down the stairs and found Roger in the kitchen making some soup.

"Hey, Roger, do you have a laptop or computer?" asked Amber.

"Yes, I do, but it is out being repaired. Sorry."

"Great!" said Amber with a disappointed look.

After thinking for a few moments, her eyes grew wide and she thought, "LIBRARY!"

"What?" asked Renalia, who watched her expression change from frustration to excitement in a blink of an eye.

"Roger, is there a library around here?" Amber asked.

"Yes, there is, it is downtown...hold it! What are you girls up to?" asked Roger suspiciously.

"We need to look something up," replied Amber, "In America, libraries don't just have books, they also have computers where you can look up information."

Roger thought for a moment, then said, "Oh, all right, but just make sure you get back here for dinner. You can stay for dinner as well, if you would like, Renalia."

"Oh, I would love to, thank you, Roger," she replied.

"By the way, how do we get to the library?" asked Amber.

"When you walk out the door, take a left and walk to the corner. There will be a bus stop sign right there. They have a set schedule and a map," said Roger looking at the clock, "And at this rate, if you run, you just might make it."

"Thanks, Roger!" exclaimed Amber, heading out the door.

The girls rushed out the door and ran to the bus stop. They arrived just in time, for the bus had pulled up to the curb. Once they boarded, Amber realized she had no money, but Renalia said, "That is okay, I have change." After she paid the driver, they quickly sat down and the bus started off. After a few moments Renalia said, "There is also one more thing I forgot to mention. My parents do not know I am here. Actually, they still think I am at home."

Amber turned and looked at Renalia, "What?!" she exclaimed.

"Well, they have been making sure that I do not get out of the house," said Renalia.

"Why would that be?" asked Amber who was now more mystified than ever.

"I have absolutely no idea," she replied.

Amber sat and thought for a moment. "Well, I have a few questions then. How did you mail the letter to me, how do you know Adalard and how did you get out of the house without getting caught?"

"That was the tricky part," said Renalia deep in thought, "Both times I had to make sure my parents were either asleep or not home. I climbed out of a window that has a strong vine next to it that grows up the side of the house. And as for knowing Adalard, I snuck a peek at the newspaper and saw how you and your cousins solved that mystery. I was able to find his contact information in the phone book while my parents were out and he suggested I talk to you."

"Oh," said Amber.

Chapter 2

A Conspiracy

"So where's the library?" asked Amber. They had just climbed off the bus and were looking at their new surroundings.

Renalia looked around and pointed down the street, "Maybe that one?" she said, pointing to a large building that had large columns in front of it and statues of horses on either side of the entrance.

Amber gaped at the building she pointed out and said, "Yeah, that sorta does look like a library. Let's go check it out."

The girls headed towards the building and stopped at the bottom of the steps. "Wow! It's huge!" said Amber, "there must be a ton of books in here. Wonder if they have computers, too." They walked up the steps and entered the building. As they passed through the doorway and into a narrow hall the air suddenly became cooler.

"It smells like old books in here!" said Amber.

"Well, of course!" said Renalia with a slight grin.

As they reached the end of the hall they entered a large round room with a high domed ceiling. On the ceiling was a beautiful painted mural of cherubs that looked as if they were singing. The wooden floors showed that many people had walked in there. There were three other doors leading to hallways that exited the room, almost like the four points of a compass. Except for the beautiful Greek statues at each door and the circular reception desk, the room was bare. A young girl sitting at the desk was focused on what appeared to be paperwork.

"Excuse me, but do you have computers here for public use?" asked Amber.

The young girl looked up from her paperwork, pointed to a doorway, smiled and replied, "Go down that hall, take a right and the last door on your left will be the computer room."

"Thank you," replied Renalia.

The two teens headed off in the direction the young girl pointed to and finally came to a large circular room with many computers along the walls. Because it was getting late, the room was completely empty except for the two girls.

Amber ran to the nearest computer and immediately began searching. Renalia pulled up a chair right next to her, for she didn't know what to look for. After a while Amber said, "Renalia, I hate to say this but I can't find a thing! It's like someone erased your records! Either that or didn't put them in!" She looked through a few more web sites and as she did, she became a little more concerned. "You're definitely right, something is terribly wrong."

Amber got up from the computer, stretched, looked at Renalia and said, "Let's go back to Roger's place. By the time we get there, it will be dinner."

They set off and after twenty minutes they were eating some of the greatest soup they'd ever tasted.

"Thank you, Roger! That was really good!" said Renalia.

Amber smiled in agreement, then asked,

"Roger? Can a person erase someone's birth records?"

"Not very easily, but I think only the queen or someone with her authority can do that," he replied, "Why do you ask?"

"Because we couldn't find Renalia's birth records. We tried searching for them!" explained Amber.

Roger had an odd look on his face as he replied, "Maybe it is a computer glitch, or someone overlooked it."

Amber thought about all of this information, and then asked, "By the way, who's the queen?"

"Her name is Queen Rose. Unfortunately she is dying. She is very sick and has been for quite a while. Some people think it is because of the death of her daughter. Her oldest niece, Princess Kaleya, will be taking the throne. I think she is in her mid thirties," said Roger.

"How come I have never heard of this woman?" asked Renalia.

"Do you not watch the tely or read the newspaper?" questioned Roger.

"No, we do not have a tely and my parents hide the newspaper, so I do no get to read it often," replied Renalia.

Both Roger and Amber stared at the girl. Amber thought it was odd that Renalia wouldn't have much access to two of the most common news sources on the planet. There was no other place to turn. It was as if Renalia never existed!

"I know this sounds crazy, but I have a feeling your parents are conspiring against you," said Amber.

"That is not crazy at all," replied the girl, "What should we do now?"

Amber thought for a moment and then said, "Hmmm, I think I have an idea. Renalia, is it possible we could go to your house?"

"Yes, we could. I do not think my parents are home, but why on earth would you want to go there?"

"We might find some clues there," replied the young sleuth. "Roger, we'll be back in a little bit."

"Okay, but I am not too sure about this, Amber..." he replied.

Before he could even finish his sentence the girls were out the door.

It took two bus rides to get to Renalia's house but when they arrived they had to walk down a few more streets and finally came upon a lovely white mansion. There were rose bushes surrounding the front of it, and there were large vines with yellow flowers climbing up the sides.

"Renalia, your house is magnificent!" exclaimed Amber.

"Thank you, but it is not so magnificent if you are stuck in there all day long," replied the girl sadly, " Come on, we do not have much time. Let us go into my parent's office, there is bound to be something in there."

They ran around the side of the house and climbed up the large thick vine. Once they reached the opened window, they crawled through and walked down the hall to a half opened door. The door opened into a beautiful room, which Amber assumed to be the study. It had one large window and a large chandelier. Under the chandelier was a mahogany desk with dozens of papers and letters scattered about. "Looks like they left in a hurry!" commented Amber.

"This is how they normally leave things here," replied Renalia.

"Let's get to searching!" exclaimed Amber, already rummaging through a pile of important documents.

■ ■ ■ ■ ■ ■ ■ ■ ■ ■ ■ ■ ■ ■ ■ ■ ■

"I cannot seem to find anything except a bunch of letters!" exclaimed Renalia in frustration after about an hour of searching. She threw some letters to the floor. As they fell on the carpet, one letter caught Amber's eye. It was a white envelope and on the back was what looked to be a royal seal! Amber picked it up and opened the letter.

"Renalia? Did your parents have connections with the queen?" asked Amber.

"No, not that I know of," she replied.

"Isn't this the queen's seal?" asked Amber.

"I am not sure, but we can find out," said Renalia.

"Let's read what it says, shall we?" said Amber.

February 21, 2008

You two had better be careful to not give Renalia the slightest clue as to who she is. If she even gets a glimpse of me she will instantly remember! You must do everything in your power to keep her locked up until my coronation. Most importantly, you must make sure she never finds the silver chest! If she does my plans will be ruined and if that happens you two will have nowhere to hide! I will make that a promise.

Your future queen,
Princess Kaleya

"Oh my! My parents are conspiring against me! With the princess! What does this Kaleya person have against me anyway?" questioned Renalia who seemed to be afraid.

"I don't know, but I believe our best bet would be to find that silver chest," replied the sleuth.

"Amber, take a look at the rest of the letter," said Renalia.

Amber looked at Renalia in confusion then noticed a "P.S." at the bottom of the page. It read:

P.S. One more thing, Renalia is a very smart girl and I am sure she knows who Amber Oak is. From what I hear, Amber is a young American girl who enjoys solving mysteries and she is quite good too. If this does happen I do not care what the cost is, just get rid of Amber Oak! She is the only one that can get in my way right now.

Amber read that portion of the letter over and over again. "Renalia, we need to find as many of these letters as we can, just look for the royal seal," said Amber.

Renalia did as Amber said and they each grabbed a handful of letters.

"I have found more, Amber!" exclaimed Renalia. As soon as she spoke, a car door was heard from the driveway below.

"Oh no! They are back! We are so dead!" exclaimed Renalia in a panic.

"Renalia, pull yourself together. We'll just escape through the window and grab a bus back to Roger's place," said Amber, shaking Renalia back to her senses.

Renalia nodded and they quickly made their way to the window. "Wait! What about my clothes?!" asked

Renalia. "Don't worry about them! I think I have plenty of stuff that might fit you," whispered Amber.

She quietly opened the window and, grabbing hold of the vine, started to descend to the ground.

Renalia then slowly made her way down the vine. Suddenly she lost her footing and slid the rest of the way down the vine scraping her hands in the process.

"Renalia, are you all right?" asked Amber worriedly. Renalia nodded and replied,

"I am fine, but my hands are not!"

Amber took Renalia's hands and examined them. They were scraped, but not badly.

"You'll be okay until we get to Roger's house," said Amber, "Do you still have the letters?"

Renalia nodded.

"Should we tell Roger about this?" asked Renalia as the two girls raced to the bus stop.

"Yes, believe it or not, I think he can definitely help us now," replied Amber.

The bus took a while to get to the stop, which gave the girls a few anxious moments. But to their relief the bus finally came around the corner and they were soon on their way to Roger's house.

Chapter 3

Danger

As the girls rode along on the bus they discussed the matter at hand.

"Hey, Renalia, read this letter," said Amber handing a piece of paper to her.

Renalia took it and read:

June 15, 2008

For the last time I will tell you what I plan to do when I am queen. I plan to make Galacia the most powerful nation in the world and everyone will worship and adore me! But of course Renalia must be eliminated first!

Your Majesty,
Princess Kaleya

"Oh my gosh! This cannot be! I never did anything to her!" exclaimed Renalia in tears.

"Renalia, you probably didn't do anything …well, intentionally," said Amber calmly.

"Then…why does her majesty want me exterminated?" asked Renalia between sobs.

"I don't know, Renalia, but we're going to find out," said Amber, "I assure you."

The girls were so caught up in the mystery that they almost missed the stop for Roger's house. They jumped off the bus and didn't stop running till the door closed behind them.

"Where in the world have you two been? I thought you were just going to Renalia's house. Renalia, why are your hands bleeding?" questioned Roger.

"It's kind of a long story, Roger," replied Amber.

"Well, we have got all the time in the world," replied Roger who seemed pretty tense.

Amber spilled the entire story, knowing deep down inside that Roger might not believe them.

"Yeah, right, her majesty would not do such a terrible thing!" exclaimed Roger, who expressed shock at their tale.

"If you do not believe us, then read these letters!" replied Renalia in frustration.

Roger took the letters from Renalia's hands, which made her wince a bit. As he read them, his eyes widened and then he replied, "I am sorry girls, I am sorry for not believing you! How, may I ask, do you expect to stop this terrible conspiracy?"

"We don't know, we were hoping you could help us," replied Amber.

"I do not know either, but do not worry at all, Renalia, we will protect you. Believe me. Let me take a look at your hands," replied Roger, "Hmm, the scratches are getting infected. I will go get the first aid kit."

Roger went into the next room and quickly came back with a huge box. As Roger wrapped Renalia's hands he asked, "So you have no idea of why Princess Kaleya would be after you?"

Renalia shook her head no.

"Well, I am willing to help you girls. You have my full support and if I think of anything I will let you know," replied Roger.

Amber smiled and suggested that she and Renalia go to the library the next day and search for some more info.

"You do not have to wait that long, Amber, the shop where I brought my computer to be repaired called to tell me that it was fixed, so I went and picked it up," said Roger, " I put it in your room."

Amber and Renalia went to Amber's room.

"Amber, what exactly are we looking for?" asked Renalia.

"I'm trying to look for information on this silver chest... and I think I've got it," replied Amber.

Renalia leaned over Amber's shoulder and looked at the screen then replied,

"The legendary silver chest? Okay, I am officially confused. If it is legendary then why is Princess Kaleya fretting that I will find it?"

"Maybe it isn't legendary. What if it's real and she made it sound like a legend just as a precaution? What if she knew we might find it? Wait a second, if she is in control of Galacia, she must have sources that can erase birth records and recreate certain files," said Amber as her mind flew from one thought to the next.

"Sorry, girls, could not help but overhear," said Roger, appearing in the doorway.

"What are we going to do, Roger? We're coming up with dead ends!" exclaimed Amber in obvious frustration.

"Do not give up, girls! I am sure there is something that we have not thought of yet, now let us think..."

"Hold on, remember in one of the letters how the princess said that if I got a glimpse of her that I would recognize her the second I saw her?" said Renalia in a thoughtful tone.

The other two nodded and Renalia continued, "Do you happen to have a picture of her?"

"Yes I do, I will go and get it," said Roger as he left the room. He returned and handed a newspaper to Renalia.

Renalia stared at the image of the Princess and her eyes did not leave the page for quite sometime. Then she spoke up and said,

"I know who this woman is and of course I have heard of her..." she started. Her eyes widened as she exclaimed, "but I have other memories of her! How can that be when I have never met her?"

Amber thought about this for a moment. This was probably one of the most confusing mysteries she had ever attempted to solve. "Renalia, what are the memories you have of her? Can you remember anything else at all?"

Renalia sat down on the bed deep in thought, "I remember this woman's face, but she was a lot younger." She thought for a moment longer then said, "I remember something about roses also, and her face and the roses seemed to go together." Then something dawned on Amber and she asked, "Renalia, is it possible you remember her from your childhood?"

"I suppose it is possible, but I do not know why and that still leaves us with hardly any clues!" replied the distressed girl.

"Hey, Amber, do you not have any connections back in the States?" asked Roger.

"What do you mean?" she replied.

"Do you not have friends that could find out more information on Princess Kaleya and this silver chest?"

Amber's expression changed from being upset to happy. She ran out of the room and as the other two started to follow her she ran back into the room and asked, "Roger, where's your phone?"

"It is downstairs in the kitchen," he replied. They all ran down stairs with Amber in the lead. She reached for the phone and quickly dialed a number.

"Hey, Matt," said Amber, " this is Amber. How are you doing?"

"I'm doing pretty good, how about you?" he replied.

"I'm doing okay. Hey, can you do me a favor? Could you put your computer skills to the test? Wait, hold on, let me put you on speaker," said Amber, "Okay, I need you to look up something."

"Go for it, I'm online," said Matt.

"Can you look up something called the silver chest that's related to the country called Galacia?" asked Amber. "Sure, just give me a minute," he said. In a moment he replied, " I keep getting prohibited sites. Hold on, let me try something else." After a few moments he said, " I've just hacked into one of the legendary sites. I'm not sure why, but it looked kinda strange. I'll try to find out who posted it."

"Princess Kaleya, no doubt. Please, Matt, this is a matter of life and death! I need to know if it's real and if it is, I need to know where it is!" exclaimed Amber.

"Okay! Okay! Patience!" said Matt, "from what I can tell... if it is real, which at this point is highly debatable, its kept somewhere hidden.

"Is there anything else, Matt?" asked Amber.

"Um...yeah...it's really hard to find, there are tons of traps guarding it or something. To be honest, sounds really sketchy to me. If you're trying to find it, Amber, I wouldn't. It sounds really dangerous too. Whoever posted it, probably doesn't want anyone finding it. Just a friendly word of warning."

"Thanks Matt, anything else?"

" Nope but I...Uh oh, my dad wants the phone. He can get really hasty at times. Sorry."

"That's okay, I'll talk to you later!"

"Bye, Amber. Hope you solve this mystery if that's what you're doing."

Amber hung up as she turned to her friends and said, "Any ideas?"

Renalia thought for a moment then said, "I am not sure, without any tips, we have nothing."

Amber sat down on the bed with her hands covering her face. Then an idea hit her. "I got it! The elderly!"

"What about the elderly?" asked Renalia.

"I was always told that behind every myth and legend there is some truth. So think about that. Usually legends are very old, so if this silver chest is a legend, then maybe the elderly of Galacia will know something about it!" explained Amber in excitement.

"I guess that is a possibility, that is if Princess Kaleya has not threatened them to not say anything about it," said Roger negatively.

Amber rolled her eyes and stared at Roger, "Roger, this is the only lead we have, unless you have a better idea." He shrugged his shoulders in response. "So, what are we waiting for? Let's go!" said Amber.

Chapter 4

The Silver Chest

"What?! We cannot go out now! It is way too dark!" said Roger.

"I guess you're right," said Amber, "we'll wait." She froze for a moment as another thought came to her. " Just out of curiosity, when is Princess Kaleya's coronation?" asked Amber.

"Oh, it is on Saturday," replied Roger.

"WHAT?! That's only two days away!" exclaimed Amber, "not only that, but my idea is just a theory!

"Well, it is your idea, detective!" said Roger walking away. Amber sighed in frustration. Renalia put a hand on Amber's shoulder and said reassuringly, "I believe it is a fantastic idea. Roger is probably just tired he is just losing hope. It is worth a shot!"

"I certainly hope you're right," replied Amber.

■ ■ ■ ■ ■ ■ ■ ■ ■ ■ ■ ■ ■ ■ ■

"Who should we ask first?" asked Renalia as soon as they got to the city the next day. Amber looked around and said, "Well, we have a lot to choose from and we should also be careful because Kaleya may have talked to some of the elderly."

"Good point, I did not think of that," replied Renalia, "Shall we split up or stay together?"

Looking around the foreign area, Amber replied, "Just to be on the safe side, we should stick together."

They went to many different people, but found no leads. "Is that all the elderly?" asked Roger.

"Excuse me! I could not help but overhear you asking some people about a silver chest?" said an old man in the shadows.

"Yes. We are trying to find it. That is, if it exists," replied Amber, who seemed very uncertain about this mysterious old man.

The old man laughed and coughed, "Why yes my dear, it does exist!"

"Really! Oh my! That is the best news we have heard all day! Where on earth is it? Do you know?" asked Renalia.

He came out of the shadows a little bit and said, "I do know where it is, but to reach this chest, is a treacherous journey. You must endure many challenges and obstacles and solve numerous amounts of riddles to reach your final destination."

"Sounds easy enough," said Amber.

"Oh, but be forewarned, this is not an easy task. Many have died trying to get it. Many have gone mad! Good luck to you," said the old man returning to the shadows.

"Uh, would you mind telling us where to start?" asked Roger.

The old man turned and stared at Roger for a long time, then replied, "Journey to the West, there thou shalt find thy quest."

They walked away from the old man and Roger said, "I think that man has lost a few marbles. Who agrees?"

Amber couldn't stop thinking about what the man meant about finding their quest in the West, "I don't think he lost them, I think he means that maybe what we're looking for is in the west or in that general direction. Let's take a look at a map."

"Good thing I brought one from the house!" said Renalia.

Amber opened up the large map of Galacia and looked to the west, "All I see are a bunch of mountains. Does anything ring a bell to anyone?"

Renalia scanned the map and something caught her eye, "Yes, this one right here, it is the largest one it is called Mountanyan."

"What's so great about it?" asked Amber.

"I heard my parents talk an awful lot about it when I was younger, I am not sure what it was about. But it must be important, maybe we can check there?" asked Renalia.

"What have we got to lose? Let's go!" said Amber.

"Wait, girls, I am not so sure, that man was losing his mind and plus it is getting late," said Roger hesitantly.

"Roger, you can stay behind if you want. We don't have much time. We're going," said Amber firmly.

"Fine. Your brother is right about you. You are very stubborn at times!" he replied.

■　■　■　■　■　■　■　■　■　■　■　■　■　■　■

"Renalia! Roger! Hurry, we're going to miss the train!" exclaimed Amber running toward the train.

"We are coming!" replied Roger from behind.

They all jumped aboard the train and they were on their way to a place called Rosenda, for it was impossible to get to Mountanyan by train. Their timing was impeccable for moments after they got on, the train departed. The wait seemed like it went on forever when in reality it only took two hours. The wait was finally over and the trio got off and made their way to find a map of Rosenda.

"Wow, Rosenda is a bit smaller than I thought," said Amber.

"Be that as it may, where would Mountanyan be?" asked Renalia.

"Good question, shouldn't be too hard to find. It is a mountain, right?" replied Amber.

"Yes, it is, Mountanyan, in ancient Galacian, translates to snow-capped mountain," explained Roger.

"Let's go find it," said Amber.

They traveled around the small area of Rosenda for a short while and came to a steep cliff. Below was the sea, licking the jagged rocks. "Could this be the danger the old man warned?" thought Amber to herself as she stepped away from the edge. All three turned the corner and came to a little cul-de-sac. All that was to be seen, were mountains with steep slopes and cliffs at the top, which were covered in snow. "Looks like a dead end," said Renalia.

"I'm not so sure...something doesn't seem right about this," said Amber taking another look at the map, "We are in the west like the old man said. Maybe there's supposed to be a clue around here as to where the chest may be."

"For the last time, Amber. The old man was a coot!" exclaimed Roger in exasperation.

"Roger, I'm sick of your complaining! I know you're my brother's friend, but honestly, we're trying to figure out what's going on with Renalia here. Please, either go back home or help us!"

Roger was silent and continued on walking with the girls.

Amber walked towards the cliffs and examined them carefully. "Hmm, I wonder..."

"Is something the matter, Amber?" asked Renalia.

"I'm not sure...I was just thinking, this chest would be very well hidden from the public, would it not?"

"I assume so, hence why we cannot find it and hence why we look like a bunch of idiots just standing here looking at a cliff," replied Renalia.

"I have a theory. Look for a ledge of some sort along the cliffs, as small as it may be, look for any sight of one," said Amber.

Renalia gave up asking questions. She figured Amber knew what she was doing by now...or so she thought.

"That looks like a ledge over there," said Roger pointing to the left.

"So it does, let's go!" said Amber beginning to climb the steep cliff.

"Whoa! Amber! You have got to be joking! You could get killed if you are not careful!!" exclaimed Renalia in utter horror.

"Renalia, relax I have an idea, just follow my steps and we'll be fine, I've rock climbed a bit back home."

"How much is a bit in your book?" asked Roger doubtfully.

"A number of times.... look, it'll be fine, trust me. Just follow me," replied Amber reassuringly.

"Maybe this is what the old man said about danger," mumbled Roger to himself.

Renalia and Roger followed Amber up the steep cliff keeping very close to her and copying her exact movement so as to not slip. They did not dare to look down either. "Phew! We made it! That was awesome!"

"To you what may be awesome, is horrifying to me!" exclaimed Roger, brushing himself off.

"Oh, you're just a party-pooper!" said Amber with a laugh.

"Um, Amber, about that theory of yours," said Renalia.

Amber turned around and looked at her new surroundings. There was nothing of significance there!

"This is impossible!! I was sure that there was something here! Somebody must have hidden this thing really good. Let's look around."

"For what, may I ask? There is nothing here!" exclaimed Roger.

"You'd be surprised what may come up, you just have to use your eyes," replied Amber.

Roger heaved a great sigh of discontentment and walked off to one corner of the ledge.

After about fifteen minutes of searching Renalia called, "Amber! I believe I have found what you may be searching for! Come here behind these boulders!"

Amber dashed to Renalia's side and saw a decent sized tunnel going into the side of the mountain. "That's peculiar...not at all what I expected."

"Where do you think it leads to?" asked Renalia.

"Only one way to find out," said Amber.

"No way, absolutely not! I refuse to crawl on the ground like a serpent!" exclaimed Renalia in shock.

"Gosh! You sound like a princess for crying out loud!! A little dirt never hurt anyone!" said Amber.

"Must I?" whined the girl.

"If you want to find out what's in the chest and why Kaleya is after you before her coronation, then yes you do," replied Amber with a slight smile.

The girl got down on her knees and said, "Fine, let us go before anyone sees us."

"Oh yeah, I'd hate to be laughed at by the nearby seagulls!" laughed Amber, "Roger, we've found a small entrance to something; we're gonna check it out, coming with us?"

"No, I think I will stay out here, I...tend to get claustrophobic quite easily," he replied.

"Suit yourself," replied Amber.

The tunnel was incredibly long and tight, it was actually meant for a little child. How the girls managed to fit in the tunnel, neither of them knew. All they knew was the oxygen supply was very slim. "Does...this.... tunnel.... have...an....end?" asked Renalia in between breaths.

"OUCH! Yep...just found it...." replied Amber taking out her mini flashlight.

When she turned it on she was devastated! They had come to another dead end!! "You've got to be kidding me!!" exclaimed Amber. "What?! What is it?" asked Renalia from behind. "Another dead end...." replied Amber. "I do not believe it.... we could not have crawled a quarter of a mile just to come to a dead end. There must be a way to move this rock or maybe there is.... some sort of mechanism on the wall to move it? Amber, you must not give up! We have come too far to do that!"

"You're right, Renalia we must keep moving on," replied Amber. She put the mini flashlight in her mouth and used her hands as a guide to feel around the wall for a way to move the rock. Suddenly, her hand rested on one side of the wall causing the blockade in front of them to move!

"How did you do that?" asked Renalia.

"That doesn't matter at this point. What matters is keep on going," said Amber.

They had crawled into what appeared to be a large cave. With the flashlight, they examined their surroundings more thoroughly and found that there were torches along the cave wall. They appeared to not have been lit in a long time.

"This is too bizarre! Why would that small tunnel be the only way in?" asked Amber.

"I am not sure...it does seem a bit strange though, doesn't it. Perhaps we came in the back way?" suggested Renalia.

"My intuition tells me otherwise," said Amber.

They walked deeper into the cave in hopes that the flashlight would not die. The cave seemed to go on forever, that is, until they turned one corner. The sight in front of them was different; it was as if the cave went underwater. "Okay this is officially strange.... so this is what the old man meant by people went mad and that it was dangerous," said Amber.

"I know we should go on, but we do not know how far it goes. I can swim and I am sure you can as well, but, should we?" asked Renalia.

"What have we got to lose?" replied Amber.

"Um, our lives?!" said Renalia in shock.

"Oh, yeah, well... we got this far.... I think we can make it farther," said Amber getting into the water, "It's not that cold, we should be fine."

"All right, if you say so," replied the scared girl, getting in.

They dove into the freezing water and lucky for Amber her flashlight was waterproof and still worked in deep waters. Strangely enough there were tiny little fish swimming around them. "They must feed off of the algae on the floor," thought Amber to herself. Just as the girls were about to run out of breath they resurfaced and found themselves at another dead end!

"WHAT THE HECK IS UP WITH THESE DEAD ENDS?!?!" exclaimed Amber.

"Amber.... you might want to look over to your r..right..." stuttered Renalia.

"What are... oh my..." started Amber. She was speechless for in the corner was a pile of dead bodies.

"Maybe we should go back. I think we are in way over our heads now," said Renalia heading back to the water.

"No, now its personal. I'm going to find out who did this to them and why," replied Amber grabbing hold of Renalia's shirt.

"Amber, this is not your battle," said Renalia sternly.

"It may not be, but you asked me to come to Galacia to help you solve this mystery. That is what I intend to do. I NEVER leave a mystery unsolved. You can quote me on that. Come on, we're not done here."

Amber shined her flashlight all over the dead end part of the cave. To her astonishment, there was nothing to be found. Then a thought came to her. What had killed those people? She slowly went over to the pile of bodies, fearing that they could be booby trapped, but to her relief they weren't, although something else had happened to them...stab wounds were seen in many of them. "Renalia, these people were stabbed. We better hurry or whoever did this to them might come back."

Renalia nodded and helped her search the cave. "I am not finding much over here, Amber. Any luck over there?"

"No, maybe it has the same idea as the last few blockades we passed? Start examining the walls. If there is anything, it maybe hard to ident..."

"Found something!" exclaimed Renalia.

"Guess not," whispered Amber to herself. She walked over to Renalia and looked at what she found. It was a strange indentation in the wall. The young sleuth blew away the dust and wiped off as much mold as she could and the indentation appeared to be that of the royal seal!

"Renalia! This is it! This is where the chest is!"

"How can you be certain?" asked the girl.

"Hello?! The royal seal is right here! What else could it be?!" questioned Amber.

The girl shrugged, "Well, miss detective, do you have any idea what this royal seal is for or where the chest actually is?"

"No...But maybe we're close...maybe there's a door or something that we have overlooked," suggested Amber.

"Maybe it needs a key. The only question is where is the key?" said Renalia.

"No, its not a key," said Amber bending closer to the indentation, "Wait a second, there are little black dots. Hold on, let me get my magnifying glass out."

"How much can your small pocket possibly hold?" asked Renalia.

"Well it's not really a magnifying glass, its part of my pocketknife, so it's kind of small but it will still work.... that's exactly what I thought. Renalia, whatever this indentation is meant for, it requires heat, the little black dots on here are burn marks. What it needs is fire."

"Amber, in case you have not noticed, we are near water, not fire. I do not know where you are going to get fire."

"Simple," replied Amber. She got her flashlight out and put it as close to the indentation as she could, after about five minutes, it became bright red. A loud sound of gears turning came from behind the wall.

"Tada! Come on, let's go in and hope the chest is there," said Amber.

This cave was much smaller and narrower. Luckily for the girls' poor aching feet it was shorter, too. The cave came to an end but this time the end held something much more special. On a small ornate pedestal with three candles behind as the only sources of light was the legendary silver chest!!!! Amber and Renalia were so relieved. They slowly approached the chest, now afraid that a booby trap could appear for it seemed too easy. Surprisingly enough, nothing happened.

Amber stared at the small chest in amazement. She stepped up to it to get a closer look and touched the chest gently with her fingertips. She noticed the beautiful jewels on the cover as well. There were emeralds, rubies, sapphires and even diamonds! In the center of the cover was the royal crest. Amber slowly opened the cover and inside there was a royal blue color velvet with a frail piece of paper in the middle. Amber picked it up carefully because she was afraid she'd hurt it. She opened the paper and inside was writing with embellishments around the edge.

Her eyes couldn't leave the paper, but reality soon interrupted her and she said,

"It looks like a prophecy! Here's what it says:

The time shall come when evil shall take the throne of Galacia. She shall stop at nothing to obtain her lifelong desire. Yet a young princess, with the help of a foreign girl, shall stop the evil one and the magnificent one shall reign.

"Renalia, you're a princess!" said Amber bowing slightly.

Renalia was dumfounded. "How could this be?"

"The prophecy says that the time shall come when evil shall take the throne of Galacia. Now I assume that means Kaleya, and she's obviously stopping at nothing to obtaining it. Now whether it's her lifelong desire, I'm not sure, but it says a young princess with the help of a foreign girl shall stop the evil one and the magnificent one shall reign. I'm not sure about you but that certainly sounds like us and you definitely got the princess thing down," explained Amber.

"Well, if that is the case, it does explain everything, but what do we do now?" asked the baffled princess.

"Finding a way out of here is a good start," suggested Amber.

"We can always go the way we came," replied Princess Renalia.

"I'd rather we take this prophecy with us, you know, for proof," said Amber as she started looking for a way out.

"Maybe one of these candles opens a door in the wall," suggested the princess.

"I highly doubt it. Whoever made this probably..."
CLINK!

To Amber's surprise, a door immediately opened as soon at the princess pulled on one of the candles. "Oh, come on, that is sooooo cliché!" exclaimed Amber.

Princess Renalia laughed and replied, "Let us go, Miss Sleuth."

Amber shook her head in disbelief but kept on going. She was curious as to where this door would lead to; she had hoped it would lead out of all the caves.

■　■　■　■　■　■　■　■　■　■　■　■　■　■　■

"Amber, we have been walking for hours! Should we not be near the end already?"

Amber looked around to see if there were any secret doors that would allow them to lead out. "Yes, we should, let's keep going for a bit more and keep an eye out for something along the walls."

They walked along a little farther and finally managed to come back to the same area where they had originally started. "How in the world did we end up here?!" asked the princess in shock.

"Your question is about as good as mine. All I know is, if it is where we began, then let's go through the small tunnel," replied Amber getting on her knees.

"I have to crawl again?"

"I'm am sorry your highness, but with all due respect...you were the same person when you came here as and you crawled on your hands and knees, what difference does it make now that you have a new title?"

The princess heaved a heavy sigh and got on her hands and knees and they began to crawl their way to the light. However, things weren't all so light when they reached the ledge. It looked to be around dusk!

"Where is Roger?" asked Amber looking around.

"He may have went searching for us when we did not come back," said the princess.

"I don't know, something seems a bit shady now," said Amber, who was now on full alert.

"What do you mean?" asked the Princess, who was getting a bit scared.

"Haven't you noticed Roger's demeanor? Like how at times he's so eager to help us out and when we got closer to the cave he seemed more on edge."

"Yes, I suppose he did seem a bit out of sorts," replied the Princess.

"Wow, Amber, you really do know how to get yourself involved in things you should not," said a voice coming out from the rocky shadows.

"Roger, is that you?" asked Amber.

"Of course it is me, you little twit!"

"Roger, what has gotten…" started Amber, as she turned around to find a revolver pointed at her and Princess Renalia.

"What is the meaning of this, Roger?" questioned the princess in fear and anger.

"In case you have not noticed, I have been secretly working for Princess Kaleya. I have been ordered to watch you two. The princess would like to see you," he replied with a hint of maliciousness in his voice.

"I'm sure she would," Amber shot back, "you know you'll never get away with this"

"Oh, you think so, do you?" he replied, advancing forward with the revolver still in hand. The second he did that he regretted it, for Amber swiftly kicked the gun out of Roger's hand before he could shoot. As the gun spun out of reach of both of them and before Roger could throw a blow at her, she kicked the back of his knee and he fell hard on the ground.

"Kaleya did not tell me you could fight!" exclaimed Roger.

"Well, what can I say? I'm full of surprises," replied Amber.

"I am full of surprises as well, Amber Oak," replied Roger with a wicked smile.

Amber gave him a questioning look. Suddenly at the corner of her eye she saw tall, male figures dressed in black charging for her and Princess Renalia.

Chapter 5

The Phantom Daggers

Amber quickly spun around and saw five men trying to surround them. They were all carrying daggers!

"So Amber, I am sure you have heard of these men, they are the Phantom Daggers!" said Roger getting up.

Amber gasped and within a second she and the princess were surrounded. Amber knew who the Phantom Daggers were. These men were the most dangerous and elusive group of assassins known to mankind. Roger, apparently, was their leader for he continued,

"I am not going to allow my men to kill you, your highness. I will leave that to Princess Kaleya, but as for you, Amber Oak, you will perish where you stand!"

"Oh, I don't think so," replied Amber with a smirk.

Glaring at her, Roger said, "We will see."

"Men," he said looking at the five figures surrounding Amber and the young princess, "destroy this nosy, young brat, and take the Princess captive!"

The assassins did as they were told and charged for Amber. Amber knew that Princess Renalia would get hurt so she pushed her out of the way of the assassins' daggers.

"Your highness! Run! I'll take care of these idiots," yelled Amber.

Princess Renalia knew Amber was capable of defending herself, yet she just couldn't leave Amber there! With much reluctance the princess climbed up a few boulders and out of sight. As soon as the assassins started attacking, Amber strained to remember every move she could to defend herself and disable the assassins. Yet she wasn't sure whether she had enough strength to last on these men, but she had to try, for she was Princess Renalia's only hope of surviving.

Already a couple men were down, but they soon got up. Amber finally came to the realization that her moves were no match for them. Instead she used the one thing she wished she would never have to use. Her pocketknife. She never would want to hurt, let alone kill another person but in this case she had no other option unless she wanted to end up dead herself. She stabbed one and he fell to the ground, badly wounded. Concealing the knife in her hand, she jabbed another assassin in the side as he took a wild swing and missed her. "Two down and three more to go!" she thought to herself. One assassin started to run and jump at her. She ducked, as another one jumped from behind, resulting in a collision. The fifth assassin also came up behind Amber and put her in a chokehold. She quickly pinned one hand against him and was able to get her head out of his grip. As she did this she pulled his arm around to his back and pushed him away. He then made another attempt to get her. The last thing he remembered was a sharp pain in his head as Amber kicked his legs out from underneath him. Now the only one left was the head assassin himself, Roger.

He came up to Amber, as angry as ever and said, "Apparently Princess Kaleya was not the only one to underestimate you. You badly wounded all of my men! I am very impressed."

"Well, consider lesson number one learned!" replied Amber.

"What would that be?" asked Roger. Amber stepped forward and gave Roger a wicked look and replied,

"Never underestimate me, because it might be the last thing you ever do!"

"Oh, is that a threat, Ms. Oak?" asked the villain smiling.

"No, not at all, it's a promise."

Roger raised his dagger, ready to plunge it into Amber when suddenly a shot was heard and the head assassin fell down. Dead. Amber looked around for the shot hadn't come from her, then she looked up and on the top of one boulder was Princess Renalia holding Roger's revolver.

When the princess came down, Amber ran toward her and said,

"Thank you, Your Grace!"

"No, Amber, it is I who should be thanking you! You saved my life and for that I am exceedingly grateful," replied the princess with a kind smile.

"I hate to break it to you, Princess, but this battle isn't over yet!" said Amber.

Princess Renalia nodded and replied,

"Amber, do you still have the letters and the prophecy?"

Amber nodded and the two girls set off for the train.

Chapter 6

A Race Against Time

"Amber, please wait up!" pleaded the breathless princess.

"I'm sorry, your Highness, I just want to get to the queen in time. She is the only one that might be able to stop Princess Kaleya!" replied Amber with a hint of frustration in her voice.

Princess Renalia agreed and then asked, "How are we going to get to her without Princess Kaleya seeing us or stopping us?"

"Good question," replied the sleuth, "We'll just have to be very careful."

The girls jumped back on the train and waited the long two hours back.

On the way, Amber felt almost guilty of harming those men, but then she realized that they were assassins and that if she hadn't defended herself she may have ended up dead. She felt much better knowing that as soon as they explained everything to the queen, she'd put the assassins that were still alive in prison for life.

As soon as the train came to a halt, the girls jumped off and headed to a coffee shop across the street to discuss their plan.

They sat down and ordered some food and coffee and tried to figure out what should be done.

"I do not know what to do, Amber!" exclaimed Princess Renalia with a loud sigh.

"Well, we know we need to stop the coronation from happening," said Amber.

"That is obvious, but the question is how, and how do we get to the queen?" questioned the princess.

"What if we secretly enter the palace?" suggested Amber.

"That is a fantastic idea!" exclaimed the princess.

"Just out of curiosity, wasn't the coronation supposed to happen in another year?" asked Amber.

"Yes, it was, but the queen is very ill and is dying so I assume that is why they are having it tomorrow," explained the princess.

"Okay, well, I'm ready to go, are you?" asked Amber finishing her coffee. Princess Renalia nodded and the teens set out on their way to the Palace.

. . . .

"Amber, how are we going to get in there?" asked the young princess, as they crouched in some bushes near a gate behind the palace. They had circled the fence and had found that it was too high to climb over. They also heard dogs barking as they walked along and they realized if they had been able to climb over, their cover would've been blown and they might have been severely bitten. Amber was staring intently at the two guards, wishing them away.

"I'm not too sure," said Amber as she watched a truck stop at the gate. The guards looked in the back of the truck and motioned the driver through. They watched as the truck stopped and parked at an outside entrance to the Palace. "Wait a minute, did you notice that truck going into the palace grounds?" asked Amber, "Where did it come from and are there anymore?" Amber looked back down the tree-lined road and saw another truck approaching the gate. "Princess, follow me!" she said excitedly. As they ran down the road, Amber explained the plan quickly to the princess, "All we have to do is wait for another truck to come by and then jump in the back of it, and try to hide ourselves before the guards find us."

"I sure hope this works," said the princess as they hid behind some trees. After a few minutes they saw a truck approaching them and as it went by they jumped into the back of the truck.

"Look! Boxes! We could hide in them! Hurry, before the truck stops!" exclaimed Renalia.

Amber and Renalia saw two boxes that would be large enough for them to hide in. They got in quickly and just in time, for the truck came to a halt.

Amber's heart started to race. She now questioned if this plan really would work. After a few minutes she heard a guard say something that was inaudible and then the truck started to slowly move.

The vehicle came to a stop and someone opened the truck door. Both girls felt their boxes being lifted, and then someone said,

"Man, this box is heavy, I wonder what is in it."

Suddenly Renalia saw the lid to her box slowly open, but then someone said,

"Do not bother looking in the box, Ron! You might break whatever is in there!"

"Haha! Very funny," replied Ron.

Much to the Renalia's relief, Ron didn't look into the box she was in. He just got a dolly and rolled her into the palace.

"Hey Harold, what are all these boxes for anyway?" asked Ron as he walked back to the truck.

"They are for Princess Kaleya's coronation, you ding-dong!" exclaimed Harold as he dollied Amber's box out of the truck. "Come on, let us get the rest of the boxes inside."

As soon as the girls heard the doors close, Amber opened the lid a tiny bit and scanned the room they were in. "The coast is clear," she said as she opened the lid fully and got out. Renalia copied her move and joined her. "So, Amber, what do we do now?" asked Renalia. The princess looked toward Amber and saw a look of shock on her face. Renalia looked around the room and her jaw dropped, for they didn't realize how big this room was. It had a beautiful, crystal chandelier from the ceiling with gold on the frame. There were magnificent large columns in the room as well.

The floor had a beautiful red tile texture and the walls were off-white with beautiful silver flower engravings. The girls instantly felt like they had just stepped out of a fairytale book. The room looked that incredible. There was one other object in the room that caught Amber's and Princess Renalia's attention. It was a humongous throne. The frame of the throne was bronze with flowers that appeared to be roses engraved on the arms, legs, and arch of the chair. There were steps leading up to the throne and they were covered with a clean blood red carpet, which matched the velvety texture of the seat, back and armrests of the chair.

Princess Renalia just couldn't fathom the fact that if Amber's plan worked, she could be sitting in that throne quite soon. The mere thought of that picture just boggled her mind!

As the girls stood staring in awe at all of this beauty, they realized the two men were on their way back, for they heard approaching footsteps and the squeak from one of the dollies from beyond a closed door. Amber had to think quickly, for if she and the princess were caught they could end up in prison or worse! "Come on, follow me!" said Amber as she raced to the nearest door. She pulled Princess Renalia through it and closed the door just as the men opened their door and entered the room. Amber was relieved for if they were a moment slower they would have been caught.

"Hey Ron, aren't these boxes supposed to go to the church?" asked Harold, "They say, "Deliver to Church" on them."

"Oops! I guess I forgot," replied Ron.

"You are such an idiot, now we will have to bring these boxes back!" exclaimed Harold.

"Now the box is very light, that is very weird..." said Ron scratching his head.

"Hey, maybe that box made you grow some upper body strength. Come on, we do not have much time!" said Harold.

The men loaded the boxes back onto their dollies and took them out of the room.

After a few minutes the girls heard the truck start up and drive away. "I'm glad they're gone, it's getting kinda cramped in here. Let's get out of this closet and go find the queen," whispered Amber.

The girls got out, looked around the room some more and then found another doorway which opened into a long, narrow corridor that had high walls, a blue carpet and huge pictures of the royal family hanging from the walls on both sides. The frames made a beautiful contrast against the sky blue walls. Doors were spaced evenly along the walls below the pictures.

"Amber, where do we go? There are so many doors," asked Princess Renalia.

"I don't know Princess..." said Amber as she stopped abruptly.

Princess Renalia couldn't figure out what had made Amber stop until she looked at one of the pictures on the wall. It was a beautiful picture of a happy family. There was the queen, the king and a little baby girl on the queen's lap. The baby was laughing and she was very cute.

"What a beautiful family!" exclaimed Princess Renalia.

"Your Highness, maybe this is your family!" said Amber.

"I actually remember getting this picture taken! It was by a French man. I remember laughing at him because he held some sort of stuffed animal that made a weird noise every time he squeezed it!" said Princess Renalia.

"Great memory, Princess!" said a cold, wicked voice behind the girls.

The girls turned around to see a young, beautiful woman who reminded Amber of an evil fairytale character. She wore a dark blue, long-sleeved gown. Around her neck hung a black necklace with earrings to match on her ears. Her face was framed by her straight, jet-black hair, which was pulled back and trapped underneath a small silver tiara. Hanging from her forehead on a small silver chain was an onyx set in a silver frame, but what caught Amber's attention were the dark brown eyes that looked to be the eyes of the devil. Amber knew this could only be one person, Princess Kaleya!

"I knew you would be a problem, Amber Oak. I should have had my men get rid of you the moment you came here!" said the wicked princess.

"Your men are dead! Well, Roger is anyway," said Amber in defense.

Princess Kaleya glared at Amber for sometime and then yelled.

"Guards, Guards! Take these intruders to the dungeon."

Suddenly, guards appeared and surrounded Amber and Princess Renalia. As they led the young detective and the princess away, Amber yelled back, "You'll regret this!"

As soon the girls were out of site the head guard asked Princess Kaleya, "Your Excellency, what would you have me to do with the prisoners?"

"We will let the queen deal with them," she replied with an evil smile.

■ ■ ■ ■ ■ ■ ■ ■ ■ ■ ■ ■ ■ ■ ■

In the dungeon the girls were trying to find a way to escape.

"We must find a way to get out of here!" exclaimed Princess Renalia as she looked through the barred window and out to the rest of the city.

"Don't worry, if Princess Kaleya is smart enough, she'll want to get rid of us as soon as possible, right? So she'll need to tell the queen all this. The queen will summon for us, and then we'll explain," said Amber.

"It sounds too easy, Amber," replied the princess, "plus, it is our word against Princess Kaleya's!"

"Yes, but we also have evidence on our side," explained Amber.

Just as their conversation ended a guard came in and said to the girls, "The queen wishes to see you two."

The girls followed the guard and were brought to the same grand room they had first found themselves in. This time, though, the throne wasn't empty. Sitting in it was an elderly woman, wearing a pearl necklace and a beautiful ivory colored dress. She had on her head what appeared to be a silver and crystal tiara. To the left of the queen stood a tall stern looking elderly man and to her right was none other than Princess Kaleya.

After looking at them for a few long moments the elderly man said, "You may approach and bow to the queen." The girls did as they were told. After a few more moments the queen said, "Rise and tell me why you girls intruded upon my person?"

"Your Highness, we wanted to speak with you," said Amber.

"You wanted to speak with me, then why did you not request an audience?" asked the queen.

"We felt that there might be somebody here that would not want us to speak with you," replied Amber.

"Is that so?" said the queen, raising an eyebrow at Princess Kaleya, who merely shrugged her shoulders. Looking back at the two girls, she replied with all the dignity she could gather (for she was, after all, very ill), "Proceed."

The girls took turns telling the story and at times interrupting each other and talking over each other. When it was over the queen gazed at them soberly for a few moments.

Finally in a very quiet voice she said, "That is a lie! My daughter died a very long time ago! As for you two, you will suffer a horrible fate for attempting to convince me that one of you is my daughter! Remove them from our presence, Philip!"

Amber suddenly realized that the elderly man was the queen's advisor. "Wait! I have proof, your Grace!" exclaimed Amber, holding out the prophecy and the letters.

The elderly man took them and handed them to the queen.

She examined them, but then replied, "You could have easily made this up!"

The guards arrived to take the girls away but suddenly Princess Renalia spoke up and said, "Your Majesty, remember the picture of your family in that hall over there? That little baby on your lap was me! I remember that the person who took the picture was a French man and the only way to get me to laugh was a small stuffed animal that whenever he squeezed it, it made a funny noise that made me laugh." Everybody froze. The queen stared at Princess Renalia. "How could you possibly know such a thing?" asked the queen.

"It is because I remember," replied Renalia.

"This is absurd, your Majesty," started Princess Kaleya. "Please do not listen to them, they will only tell you lies..."

"Silence, Kaleya!" exclaimed the queen.

"Your Highness, if I may be allowed to speak," said Amber.

The queen nodded.

"Who told you that your daughter died and how may I ask did she die?"

The queen thought for a moment then replied, "My daughter was killed in a building that caught fire a long time ago."

"Fire? What fire, your Highness?" asked Amber.

"Pardon?" said the queen.

"Your Majesty, I do quite a lot of research on my spare time and I love Galacia and it's history, but there was no record of any building of great importance burning that involved the royal family. With all due respect, I'd imagine others could have seen Princess Renalia in the building. What makes you think she is deceased? Did you witness this?" explained Amber.

"No, I did not. Princess Kaleya told me that my daughter died..." replied the queen.

"Maybe she wanted not only you, but all of Galacia to think that Princess Renalia was dead," suggested Amber who quickly glanced at Princess Kaleya.

"I beg your pardon!" exclaimed the queen in horror.

Amber thought to herself, "I've got an idea that will prove to the queen that this is her daughter."

"Your Grace, there is one thing that doesn't add up. During that time, when this "fire" happened, wasn't Princess Renalia still a baby. If so, then how would she have gotten into that place?"

"Very true...Princess Kaleya, please explain yourself!" ordered the queen.

Everyone now looked at Princess Kaleya who turned pale. She made a run for the first door she could see.

"Guards, stop her at once!!!" ordered the queen.

Two guards came through the door and caught the fleeing princess. They led her back to face the queen.

Princess Kaleya looked up at the queen who did not look at all pleased. In fact she looked very upset!

"Explain yourself. NOW!!!" commanded the queen.

Princess Kaleya now realized that there was no one left to back her up. Her assassins were all either dead or severely injured. She finally gave up.

"Your Excellency, Renalia would not have had the capability of ruling Galacia. That is why I attempted to get rid of her. Obviously, I did not see a nosy, little detective ruining my plans."

"So it is true!? How could you have done such a horrible thing, Kaleya! How could you have possibly known that Renalia would not have made a good ruler? Why, she was only a baby!"

"It does not matter. Once I found out that you had a child, I realized that my only way to the crown was to get rid of her and to claim that she had died. I never actually planned for her to die. I hired a couple to portray Princess Renalia's parents. She never would have known that she was the Princess. Then, when Amber Oak showed up and spoiled my plan, I had to take drastic measures until my coronation was over."

"This is an outrage!!! Guards, remove Kaleya from my sight. Put her into the dungeon until I figure out what shall be done with her!" said the queen.

The guards did as they were told and walked Princess Kaleya to the dungeon.

The queen's expression softened as she looked back to the two girls. The queen motioned to Princess Renalia to come forward.

The Princess did as she was told and bowed at her feet. "Renalia, my daughter, arise and come take your place beside me," said the queen in a kind tone.

Princess Renalia went by her mother's side with a smile on her face.

"I am so glad that you are alive!" said the queen with tears now rolling down her cheeks.

"Well, mother, I would have never found you if it was not for Amber Oak."

The queen looked at the young girl who looked up at her with a nervous expression, "Amber Oak, would you please come here," said the queen.

Amber did as she was told and walked toward her.

"Well, as you girls both know, I am sick and I will pass away very soon. So I will tell parliament about this issue and that they should change their plans for the coronation. But as for you, Amber Oak, you are welcome to stay in the palace for as long as you desire and you are welcome to come to the coronation. I think that now, however, I should spend some time with my daughter and get to know her."

Amber thanked the queen and said she had to go get her things.

"Oh, there will be no need for that! I will have Philip send someone to retrieve them," said the queen.

"Thank you, Your Grace, but I must warn you, the place where my things are at is a tad bit run down. But I can give you the address," replied Amber.

"Thank you, Miss Oak, but that will not be necessary, we have already found Roger's home. We have been attempting to keep track of these Phantom Daggers, and our sources have told us that they lived in the shadier parts of Galacia," said Philip entering the room.

"How very attentive of you... Your Excellency, may I explore the castle a bit?" asked Amber shyly.

The queen smiled at Amber and replied, " Of course you may. You may even explore the castle grounds if you wish. Just be back here at five o'clock this evening. It is noon right now. You should have plenty of time."

"Thank you very much!" replied Amber excitedly. The queen nodded, Amber bowed and went off on another adventure.

■ ■ ■ ■ ■ ■ ■ ■ ■ ■ ■ ■ ■ ■ ■ ■

The castle was wonderful for a curious person like Amber. There were many passageways and corridors. To the detective's amazement, she stumbled across a grand library, which had levels upon levels of old books. "I think I'm in heaven!" she exclaimed in awe.

Unfortunately, four o'clock struck the grand clock on the wall of the library and Amber knew she should make her way back, in case she got lost. However, she had wanted to explore the castle more; after all she had only explored a tiny bit of it.

As Amber entered the throne room, she found that Princess Renalia and the queen were in the exact same place as she had left them hours beforehand.

"Did you enjoy looking around the castle, Amber?" asked the queen.

"Oh, most definitely, your Highness! This place is absolutely magnificent. I especially love your gigantic library!"

The queen gave a little laugh and then replied, "I am sure you young ladies are famished right about now."

The day had been filled with so many events that Amber didn't even realize how hungry she really was.

"There is a feast waiting for you girls. Renalia, you will also have the opportunity to meet some of your relatives. Come, follow me," replied the queen.

She slowly got up from her throne and gracefully walked down a long narrow hall that led to a large set of doors. As she approached, two servants opened the doors for them that led into a very large dining room.

Amber could not believe her eyes! Sitting around a long table in the middle of the room were a number of people. From the way they were dressed they appeared to be part of the royal family. In the middle of the ceiling hung a beautiful chandelier that appeared to have brightly lit jewels on it. There was a large, lovely fireplace at the end of the room, which had a lively fire in it. There were two large windows set in a wall on one side of the room with the moon shining so brightly through them, it didn't seem necessary to have any lights at all. On the opposite side of the room was a wall with two doors set in it, which led to the kitchens. Between the two doors were servants and maids ready to serve the queen and her guests. There was a beautifully patterned carpet underneath the table and chairs, which went well with the color of the walls. As they walked through the doors, the queen's adviser, who was standing behind the queen's chair, announced the queen's arrival. Everybody stood and bowed as they approached the table. As the adviser seated the queen, Princess Renalia and Amber waited along with everyone else while the queen took her place.

"Please, sit," said the queen, looking at Princess Renalia and Amber. The Princess sat down on the queen's right side and Amber sat down next to Princess Renalia. After they sat down the adviser said, "Everyone may be seated now."

There were a few moments of rustling, as chairs were being moved and everyone seated themselves. "I hope this goes well," said the queen to Princess Renalia, "There are other people here who had hopes of wearing the crown, aside from Princess Kaleya."

After a few moments of silence the adviser, at an unseen signal from the queen, cleared his voice and said, "Her Majesty has an announcement to make."

The queen adjusted herself and said, "As you all know, sixteen years ago I had lost my daughter in a terrible fire. I was in so much sorrow for many years. Fortunately, there had been another heir to the throne, Princess Kaleya. However, I have just received news this afternoon that Princess Kaleya has been conspiring against the kingdom." There was a shocked silence and then people started whispering and talking quietly all at once. Philip motioned for them to be quiet. She then continued, "Princess Kaleya confessed her wrong doings, yet there was more to her story. She admitted that she attempted to get rid of the child in order to obtain the crown. She devised a plan that would make sure Princess Renalia would live with a lower class family for the rest of her life. Princess Kaleya was quite smart and had planned everything thoroughly, for she made up a tall tale that Princess Renalia died in that fire. She had everyone fooled. Sixteen years later, Princess Renalia thought that something strange was happening with her "parents" yet she could not figure out what it was. She had heard about a girl of her age who lived in America and had a remarkable ability to solve mysteries. Princess Renalia was able to escape from the sight of her guardians and contact the young detective whose name is Amber Oak. Amber was very excited to help out the young Princess. These amazing young women confronted their fears and escaped danger and death, for Princess Kaleya hired the lead assassin of the Phantom Daggers to kill Amber and capture the Princess until after her coronation. Once the girls realized they were being tricked, the head assassin and his men surrounded Amber and Princess Renalia. Amber had the Princess escape while she fought these trained men. Amber was very brave for what she did. So without further ado I would like to present to you Princess Renalia and Amber Oak."

The royal family was speechless. The story seemed almost impossible to believe; yet here were the two young ladies and the royal family was certain that the queen would not make a false tale.

One man cleared his throat and asked, "May I speak, your Excellency? I have a question for Miss Amber."

The queen nodded and said, "You may."

"Miss Oak, how is it that you were able to solve this mystery, and how did you manage to make Princess Kaleya confess? I am sure she would not have done that at her own will."

Amber showed a slight smile and respectfully replied,

"Well, Sir, I do love Galacian history and I read a lot of it. When I heard of how Princess Renalia supposedly died, I just thought that something wasn't right."

"Oh, and how so?" asked the young man.

"Princess Renalia and I were brought before the queen and she had told us that Princess Renalia died in a fire. I mentioned that I research a lot and I never came across any historical evidence of any fire. If there was, it wasn't of some place of great importance. Then I also mentioned that if Princess Renalia was so young how could she have gotten into a place outside of the palace."

"You are very bright, young lady," said the young man.

Amber blushed and didn't really know what to say.

"Enough talking now, let us enjoy this wonderful feast, in honor of the heroic actions of Amber Oak," said the queen with a grateful look toward Amber.

The feast was amazing! There were all kinds of meat cooked all different types of ways such as roasted lamb, roasted beef, mutton, roasted pork, veal and rabbit. There were also different types of fowl such as swan and goose. There were plates of different types of vegetables such as turnips, parsnips, carrots, onions, leeks, garlic, and radishes. The fruit was of various types such as apples, pears, plums, cherries, and woodland strawberries.

The table was set with the utmost elegance. There was gold tableware neatly placed on the table and there were two golden candelabras near to the center of the table. Once Amber sunk her teeth into the food that she stacked onto her plate, she was immediately craving for more! Then after the dinner portion the servants served the desserts, which also came in various types, such as glazed pastries, and chocolate and vanilla cake. There were even some other desserts that Amber had never seen before, but she decided to try it anyway. After a while though, Amber had enough.

"Wow, Amber, you must have been hungry! You had three huge helpings of food," exclaimed Renalia in surprise.

Amber looked sheepishly toward the queen and to her surprise the queen and everyone around the table started laughing.

"Oh, it is quite all right my dear, I am very pleased that you enjoyed your meal."

"Now, I am sure you girls would like to meet everyone, but let us retire to the Great Luxury Room. Amber and Princess Renalia both followed the queen and everyone else followed behind. They didn't have to walk all to far until they entered the Great Luxury Room. It definitely stood up to its name. The room had a large fireplace with a portrait of Queen Rose right above it. However, there were no lights in the room. Only the fireplace and very few candles lit the room. In the center of the room was a huge sofa that appeared to have a flowered print on it. On each side of the sofa, slightly slanted toward the fireplace, were identical chairs that had the same flower print as the sofa. Amber looked up at the ceiling and noticed that there was a gold rim where the ceiling and wall met. The color of the ceiling sparkled in the glow of the fireplace as well.

The young detective sat down on the end of the couch and just stared into the fire. It looked as if the flames were dancing.

"Hello, Miss Amber!" said a young woman.

Amber looked to her right and saw a beautiful young woman wearing a lovely deep blue evening gown. She also had her hair in curls.

"My name is Cheraline. I am a Duchess, and I would love to get to know you. You are incredibly brave and not to mention, very bright, so do tell me. How did you manage to solve this mystery? Have you solved others as well?"

"Yes, I have solved other mysteries. I just love the adventure. It's really fun!" replied Amber.

"Do you not ever get discouraged or scared?" inquired the Duchess.

"I do occasionally get discouraged and at times very scared. Although I do have great friends out there for me to help me when I need it. When I'm scared, I think of the mystery I'm solving and the people I'm helping. That gets me through the struggle I'm facing. I love to help people and I do whatever I can."

The rest of the night went very well. Amber and Princess Renalia met and talked with many others. The Princess talked with her relatives and was very pleased that everything was now perfect.

After many hours of chatter and mingling, the relatives bid their farewells and went back to their mansions far off in the countryside of Galacia.

Amber and Princess Renalia both sat down on the sofa and were very exhausted.

The queen went to the girls and said, "You both have had quite a day. I will have my servants direct you to your rooms." She called to one of her servants who then led the girls to their rooms. They traveled down another long hallway, but this time instead of pictures of the royal family on the wall, the pictures were beautiful pieces of art!

The servant stopped and said something to the girls in Galacian. He bowed to the Princess and then left.

"Your Highness, what did he say?" asked Amber.

"He said that your room is across the hall from mine and that he was going to get our bags. Oh, and

Amber, from now on you have my permission to call me Renalia. I do not mind."

"Thank you Your Grac... I mean Renalia."

The servant then returned with two suitcases in hand. He put Amber's suitcase in her room and Renalia's in hers.

"I... hap... you... onjey... you... stay... miss," said the young man. As soon as he went out of hearing range Amber asked, "Renalia, does everyone know English here?" "I am not sure, but he made a very good effort to speak it, if you ask me. Well, good night Amber, I will see you in the morning."

When Renalia entered her room she was awestruck. The walls of her room were a lavender color. There was a large canopy bed with many pillows. There were large windows that had pillowed window seats. There was a huge vanity set with a matching closet.

When Amber went into her room, she too, was in awe for her room was a jade color. All of the furniture in the room matched and it was similar to Princess Renalia's room.

The young princess went back to visit with her mother while Amber just stayed in her room.

She lay down on the soft, comfy bed and rested her head on a soft pillow. Immediately her eyes shut and she was off into her dream world where nothing ever went wrong.

Chapter 7

The Coronation

Amber was woken up by a shaking sensation. She opened her eyes and saw Renalia looking at her.

"What is it, Renalia? What time is it?" asked Amber in a groggy voice.

"It is six o'clock in the morning," replied the Princess opening the massive window curtains.

"Okay, but that still doesn't explain why you woke me up this early," replied Amber, squinting as the sun shown bright in her face.

"My mother said that I must be ready for the coronation," said Renalia.

"What? When is it? Why didn't she tell us yesterday?" asked Amber stretching.

"I do not know, but I was just awakened by one of her servants and was told that my coronation is in a week and that I must prepare myself," replied Renalia.

"So you woke me up to tell me this? This is great for you, Renalia, but can I go back to bed?" asked Amber pulling the pillow over her head.

"No! You have to help me get ready for my coronation!!!" exclaimed Renalia, pulling Amber out of bed.

"It's in a week, we'll have plenty of time," said Amber getting out of bed and putting on a bathrobe.

"Oh, on the contrary, Amber, planning for a coronation is a long task. It must be perfect."

"All right, I'll help, but I don't know how much help I'll be," said Amber.

"I thought you said that you had researched Galacia," said Renalia slightly confused.

"Yeah, I did, but I haven't gotten the chance to go through all of the research. There is a bunch of information on this small country," explained Amber.

"Well, this will be more research! Only this time, it will not be from any book or computer source," said Renalia. "Get dressed and meet me in the dining room, I want to go over some things with you," said the Princess as she skipped out the door and down the hall.

Amber gave a heavy sigh and said quietly to herself, "Wow, what an interesting wake up call!"

Amber pulled on a pair of black pants and a blue sweater. She then traveled back down the long hallway and hoped that she would find her way to Renalia without getting lost.

She finally reached her destination and found Renalia sitting by her mother.

"Good morning, Amber. Did you get a good night's sleep?" inquired the queen.

"Yes, your Majesty, I did," said Amber.

"All right, Amber, we have quite a lot to do today. I hope you are up for another adventure," said Renalia with a huge smile.

Amber took a bite out of her breakfast and gave the princess a questioning look, " What are you talking about?"

"Amber, how would you like to explore more of Galacia?" asked Renalia.

"I don't know. I still have a lot of exploring of the castle to do," explained Amber.

"There will be shopping involved," said Renalia convincingly.

"What are we waiting for, let's go!" said Amber excitedly.

Both the queen and Renalia laughed.

"We will go as soon as I am completely prepared," said Renalia as she rose from her chair and headed to the double door that led out to the hall.

Amber followed after her and they both went to Renalia's room.

"Renalia, why do you need to get prepared? You are already wearing a beautiful dress," said Amber.

"Amber, there is one thing that I did not mention. I have to make an address to the country as to who I am and what has happened to me. I just hope that they believe me. I need your help as well," said Renalia.

"All right, I'll help in any way I can," replied Amber.

The princess nodded and then her two ladies in waiting came in.

"Good morning, your Highness, how may we be of service this morning?" asked one of the girls, who seemed very perky.

"You may prepare me for my announcement to the country," replied the princess, "Amber Oak will oversee and decide what looks best on me."

"Yes, your Grace," replied the other girl, who seemed pleasant but less perkier than the other one.

The girls opened the large walk-in closet and Amber walked in examining all of the gorgeous dresses. Some were long and some were fairly short. There were all sorts of dresses; light ones, dark ones, sparkly ones and some were just plain, yet all of them were still beautiful.

"What do you think the princess should wear?" asked the perkier girl.

"Hmmm, how about that one! That would look perfect! It is definitely her color," said Amber, pointing at a non-sparkly aqua colored dress with short sleeves that hung a bit off the shoulders.

"That is a very good choice Miss Amber, and what do you think should be worn with it?" asked the serious girl.

"That tiara over there would match perfectly and that silver choker with matching earrings would be very nice. Oh, and the silver colored high heel sandals would be the perfect finish," said Amber who was really enjoying herself.

The ladies in waiting took down the dress and then Amber got the jewelry and put it down on the large vanity set.

As Amber watched the ladies in waiting prepare Princess Renalia for the great announcement, she came to the realization that she really was a hero. If it wasn't for her she would never been here right now and she would possibly be dead. Renalia would have been in the hands of Princess Kaleya, which would be just as bad as dead.

"How do I look, Amber?" asked Renalia.

Amber looked at Renalia, smiled and replied, "You look just like…like a Princess!"

The Princess laughed and replied to Amber, "There is another thing that I have not told you."

Amber looked a little nervous now. What could the Princess possibly need her to do?

Renalia continued, "You will also need to wear a nice dress. I would like you to help me with making the announcement. I fear they will not believe me and it would help if you were there. I would also feel more confident."

"Are you sure? I mean, what would I say?" asked Amber who now had a reason to be nervous.

"Yes, Amber, I am sure. If I get nervous and do not know what to say I would like you to explain. After all, you have experienced the same past terrible events as I did. I might not be able to explain it all that well."

Amber took in a huge breath and replied with a slight smile, "Of course, Renalia, I will help you."

"Miss Amber, your wardrobe was already picked out for you by the Princess."

"Renalia, does your mother know what is going to happen?"

"Oh, yes, she even suggested that you should join me," she replied.

Just as Renalia spoke, the ladies came out of the closet with another pretty dress that was a light yellow color. It was short and it had spaghetti straps with a matching jacket, and high heels.

"You will look very beautiful, Amber," replied the Princess.

The ladies in waiting got Amber ready as well. Then the royal hairdresser came in and made the girls look even more beautiful.

Once the royal hairdresser left, Renalia said, "Are you ready to speak with the press and the country?"

Amber nodded. As she and Renalia walked down the long hallway, butterflies started fluttering around in her stomach. When they entered another large room, Amber saw a massive amount of people, with cameras, and notebooks, basically the whole nine yards.

She and Renalia took their places up near the podium. Amber then sat down next to Renalia, and the butterflies started to flutter even faster. She had never been this nervous before!

Renalia got up and approached the podium. She stood up straight and tall and then spoke, "Good afternoon and thank you for coming. I have an announcement to make. Many of you know that sixteen years ago a young princess was born, Princess Renalia, and a little while later she died in a dreadful fire. I must tell you that you have been given false information. I am here to tell you today that I am Princess Renalia."

After a moment everyone started talking at once.

"Please, one at a time!" said Renalia.

"That is not possible," said one reporter. " Princess Kaleya is the true princess," said another. " Yes, she told us that the Princess Renalia died in the fire," said another reporter near the back.

Renalia froze. She wasn't sure what to say next, but then Amber got up and came to Renalia's rescue.

"Princess Kaleya lied to you. Princess Renalia never died but was simply taken away and was raised up by an adopted family. Princess Kaleya's plan was to get rid of the young Princess, but never to kill her. She just wanted to put Princess Renalia away until after her coronation. The villainous princess admitted to the queen what she had done."

"Can you prove it?" asked a female reporter.

Amber now got very argumentative and asked,

"Okay then, answer me this, did anyone actually see this fire happen? Why weren't you reporters at the scene? Plus, if Princess Renalia was so young, then how could she have gotten out of the castle?"

The reporters started talking amongst themselves. Then another replied, "Be that as it may, I personally would like to see some proof of your tale."

"All right, if you think Amber is lying then hear it straight from the source!" said Renalia pointing toward a door.

Out of the door came two guards leading the former Princess Kaleya up to the podium.

She looked out to the audience with chains dangling from her wrists and with tears streaming down her face. Speaking softly, she said, "What this nosy little American claims... is correct. This is the true Princess Renalia. She never deserved that crown but I did, I was the oldest, I had the country's best interest at heart."

"Oh, and what was that, Kaleya? Becoming a dictator and commanding everyone to do everything you say?" questioned Amber.

Kaleya gave Amber a malicious look and screamed, "AMBER! YOU RUINED EVERYTHING! ALL MY PLANS FOR THE PAST SIXTEEN YEARS RUINED!!! YOU ARE A MEDDLING LITTLE BRAT AND I WILL SOON GET MY REVENGE. JUST YOU WAIT!!!!"

The guards took Kaleya away and Amber spoke to the crowd, "Now do you believe me?"

The reporters didn't say anything for a moment. Then one young women spoke up and asked, "How did this happen? How did you get Kaleya to confess?"

"Kaleya knew that she was caught. There wasn't much she could do. So she finally admitted defeat," explained Amber.

Princess Renalia said, "Kaleya hired the most infamous group of assassins in the world, the Phantom Daggers. They were ordered to come after me and take me to the palace to be thrown into the dungeon. I was doomed, that is, until my best friend, Amber Oak, came in and saved my life and, more importantly, saved our country from the hands of an evil tyrant. I owe her my thanks." The whole room went silent. Then, out of the blue one reporter stood up and started clapping. Then more and more people followed and before Amber knew it, the entire room applauded her for her brave acts.

■ ■ ■ ■ ■ ■ ■ ■ ■ ■ ■ ■ ■ ■ ■ ■

The girls went out into the palace garden after the reporters left and sat down on a large white wooden swing. As they sat there, Amber looked around and saw that beautiful rose bushes bordered the garden. In fact, most of the garden held rose bushes. Some roses were pink, orange, red, yellow, and some were even multicolored, something you would not find in America! The bushes appeared to be well taken cared of. There were also some trees that had a green-orange colored fruit.

"This is such a beautiful place!" exclaimed Renalia.

"I agree. So now that the big announcement's over, what will we do?" asked Amber.

Renalia thought for a moment and then replied, "It is a little too late to start shopping. I was thinking that we make plans for tomorrow and figure out what we will do. We can also think of how the coronation should be set up. One thing is for certain; I will not have my coronation in a church. I would like it to be here at the palace."

"Absolutely!" said Amber.

"For now, let us go and see if there is any room in the palace that is appropriate for the coronation," suggested Renalia.

Renalia got up and started walking back to the palace and Amber followed after.

The two teens spent the rest of the night exploring the palace to find the perfect room.

"Amber, we have looked everywhere, there is no other room except for the throne room!" said Renalia in a discouraged tone.

"Don't give up, Renalia! I'm sure we can find something!" said Amber.

Amber traveled down a hallway that they didn't explore yet and then she yelled back to Renalia, "Hey, I've found a perfect room!!!"

Renalia followed Amber and entered into an enormous rectangular room. It looked similar to the throne room but it seemed more fancy. There were two columns toward the end, one on each side and spaced out from the wall a little bit. The floor was laid out with light colored tiles. It also had silver lined borders separating the walls from the ceiling.

"This is a great room! The throne can be placed at the other end. Hmmm... the columns can be decorated as well! This is amazing and it is much larger than the throne room!" exclaimed Renalia with a huge grin on her face.

■ ■ ■ ■ ■ ■ ■ ■ ■ ■ ■ ■ ■ ■ ■

The rest of the week went by really quick, for the girls traveled all around Galacia looking for things for the coronation. They shopped for make-up, jewelry, gowns, and shoes. The hardest part was to find what they would need for the coronation.

Unfortunately, all the fun had to end, for the big day came.

It was in the late afternoon and the coronation was going to start at any moment. Amber wasn't able to help Renalia out with getting ready, but she did take her place near the front of the large audience. She had been given a special honor. Only people of royal or noble class were allowed to come. She gazed back down the red carpet that stretched from the throne to the double doors where two doormen stood.

Suddenly trumpets sounded and everyone looked toward the entrance where the doormen were slowly opening the doors. Right in the doorway standing side by side was the queen and a beautiful young princess. A little off to the side of the queen stood Philip, her adviser, who announced in a loud voice, "Attend, all ye here, the queen of Galacia has come!" Everyone bowed as the queen and princess paused for a moment, and then started to walk toward the throne. The princess wore a very gorgeous red gown with a long train with golden glitter and jewelry. Her hair was up in beautiful curls with a golden tiara placed neatly on her head.

She walked up to the throne and gracefully sat down. The queen, who was standing beside the throne, looked out over the audience with a look that commanded silence.

"My good people, I am in ill health and for that reason, my daughter will become your new queen today." She took off her crown and, looking at Princess Renalia, said, "Will you promise to follow the laws of Galacia and protect the people?"

The princess had a happy tear trickle down her cheek and replied, "I will."

The queen placed the crown on Renalia's head and said, "Ladies and Gentlemen, I present to you your new queen, Queen Renalia!"

The former queen stepped away as the new queen rose from the throne. As Queen Renalia stood and looked out over the people, Amber thought to herself, "Wow, she looks more like a queen than she does a princess."

"All bow to the new queen!" said the adviser as he took his place beside the new queen. As Amber bowed she caught a glimpse of Renalia who gave her a little smile.

"All rise!" intoned the adviser. The trumpets sounded, the people bowed once more and then the new queen left, followed by the former queen, the royal family, the nobles and last but definitely not least, Amber.

After the coronation feast, Amber didn't know what to do at this point so she went back to her room and changed into a pair of blue jeans and a purple short sleeve shirt. She then grabbed a book out of her suitcase.

A knock on the door startled Amber and she replied, "Come in."

"Hello, Amber, I would just like to thank you for everything that you have done," said Renalia, who now wore a casual dress.

"It was my pleasure," replied the detective.

"I have a lot of duties to attend to already, including helping my mother. Unfortunately, you and I really cannot do that much right now, but I promise you, we will be able to spend some time with each other," said Renalia.

"Oh, I understand completely, plus I'd like to see how my book ends. If you need anything at all I will be glad to be of service," said Amber with a smile.

The queen nodded and exited the room.

Amber sat back down on the windowsill and put her book aside. She considered what had happened in the past events.

"Maybe Chris was right, maybe my life is getting too serious," said Amber to herself looking up at the starry night sky, " Maybe I should give up mysteries before I get killed!"

Amber went to bed that night with so much on her mind. She couldn't figure out what to do. Should she take a break from all the mysteries or should she continue to solve them?

The next day, after breakfast, Amber went out into the garden and sat on the swing. Instead of reading she just relaxed and closed her eyes. Her focus was mainly on the surrounding sounds. She heard birds flying overhead and smelled the combination of roses and fresh mowed grass. Then a sudden sound of crying approached her. She quickly jumped up from the swing and saw Queen Renalia running toward her.

"Renalia, what's wrong?" asked Amber.

The young queen ran to Amber and gave her a hug. "My mother has passed away!!" Amber hugged her back and replied, "I am sooo sorry!"

"My mother wanted the funeral to be small. She did not want it to be a big ordeal," replied Renalia looking up to Amber.

"Well, we must respect your mother's wishes. I assume the press will be there?" asked Amber.

Renalia dried her tears and replied, "We will try to prevent them from coming, yet the entire country will find out the terrible news soon."

Amber nodded. She, at this point, was at a loss for words. What could she do, other than feeling sorry for Renalia.

Several days later the funeral took place. It wasn't as small as the queen wanted, but it was of a decent size. The royal family had their own cemetery on top of a beautiful hill that overlooked the palace and a good part of Galacia.

The casket was carefully placed in the ground and Amber looked up to see the grand tombstone. It was really tall and the face of the former Queen Rose was carved into it. Below the face was written:

Her Excellency Queen Rose
She was an exceptional ruler, well loved by her subjects and will be profoundly missed.
1940-2009

A few days after the funeral, Amber and Queen Renalia were walking the palace grounds.

"Amber, before my mother died, we talked about you. She and I agreed that you should be rewarded for your acts of heroism."

"Renalia, you don't have to. I just wanted to help, it's okay."

"Amber, no, I insist. Please, it would mean a lot to me and to my mother. We both decided that your day will take place on December 1st."

Amber smiled and replied, "All right, I don't know what to say."

"Amber, you do not have to say anything. It is my pleasure."

▪ ▪ ▪ ▪ ▪ ▪ ▪ ▪ ▪ ▪ ▪ ▪ ▪ ▪ ▪

With all of the preparation going on, Amber knew she had to take a break and call her brother so that he knew what had happened. Amber asked Queen Renalia where she could find a phone.

"Oh, there should be a telephone around here somewhere…hmmm. You could see if there is one in the entry hall. Amber, if you would like, you may allow your brother and some friends to join us. They need not to worry about the expenses of the plane trip here and back. I would gladly take care of that," said the young queen as she looked at some fancy decorations for the upcoming event.

"Great, thanks!" said Amber as she went to the hall.

Once the young sleuth reached there, she looked around and saw a telephone sitting on a small table with a marble top.

She quickly dialed the number and was glad to hear the sound of her brother's voice.

"Hi, Chris!!!" she exclaimed.

"Hey kiddo, I haven't heard from you in a while! Is everything okay over there? Did you solve that mystery involving that girl yet?"

"Actually, she's now a queen and yes, I did solve it. You're not gonna believe what I've been through," replied Amber.

"Whoa, hold it. Queen?" said Chris in a confused voice.

"It's quite an interesting story," said Amber innocently.

"Tell me all about it, I'm not busy!" replied Chris who seemed interested already.

Amber told him every single detail and when she finally finished, there was silence on the other end of the phone.

"Chris? Are you still there?" asked Amber.

"Yeah, I'm still here. I can't believe it. How could Roger do that? I mean, he was one of my best friends. So, um, when you coming home?" asked Chris who, by the sound of his voice, was still in shock by the disturbing news.

"See, that's the part I kind of left out," said Amber.

"Oh, great, there's more to this story? Will I like it?" asked Chris.

"Actually, you will. Queen Renalia wants to reward me for saving her and her country and she says it's okay if you come along! Some of my friends as well," explained Amber.

"Amber, we don't have that kind of money on us. I'm sorry, I don't think I'll be able to make it," said Chris in an apologetic tone.

"No, Queen Renalia said that she will take care of that!" said Amber.

"Oh, well then, I'll be over there as soon as possible! By the way, who else do you want to come along?"

Amber rattled off the names of a couple of people.

"All right! I'll tell them about the situation and I'm sure they'd be glad to come! When do we arrive at the airport?"

"Hmmmm… I don't know but when I find out I'll call you back!"

"All right Amber, be careful! Don't go getting yourself into more trouble!! Love ya, sis!"

"Bye!" she replied.

As soon as Amber hung up the phone she ran back to Renalia and told her what her brother said.

"Oh, your brother and your friends should be at the airport at seven o'clock in the morning on November 28th. This way they will be able to explore the castle and they can get settled in as well," explained Renalia.

"Okay, thanks. I'll let Chris know," said Amber, running back to the entry hall.

Amber called Chris back and told him what the plan was. He said that that would be okay and he had already talked with Amber's friends and their parents and it was perfectly fine with them.

Amber couldn't wait for them all to come! She knew that they'd arrive in a couple days but it would still feel like forever!

The young sleuth and queen spent the next day deciding what else should be done. The invitations had already been sent and the food for the party afterward was already decided. There was going to be music and much more mingling!

"Now, what do we do, Renalia?" asked Amber sitting in a big fluffy chair.

"Now, we may do what ever you would like," she replied.

Amber thought for a moment. She wanted to do so much, but where to start, was the big question, "I'd like to see more of Galacia's historic sites. That would be cool!"

"Absolutely!" said the queen with excitement in her voice.

The girls went all over Galacia for the rest of the day and that night Amber could hardly sleep! She then realized that if she fell asleep the morning would come sooner.

The next morning Amber woke up and jumped out of bed. She could hardly wait to go greet her brother and her friends. She threw on some clothes. At this rate she didn't even care if the clothes matched.

Amber walked out of the palace where she found a limo waiting for her! "Sweet! I've never been in a limo before," she said to herself as she got in.

As the limo started off, Amber couldn't sit still, she was so excited, but within a short amount of time they arrived! She quickly got out of the vehicle and saw the plane! She jumped up and down excitedly! When she saw the passengers come off the plane she ran as fast as she could toward them.

"CHRIS!!!!!!" shouted Amber in great excitement.

The girl ran to her brother and gave him a HUGE hug! "I missed you so much!!!" she said almost in tears. She then saw her friends and they all gave her a group hug. "Amber! Chris told us everything! How did you manage to do it?!" asked her friend Megan.

"I'll tell you everything when we get back to the palace," replied Amber.

"What? Palace? Chris didn't mention we'd be staying in a palace," said Justin, Amber's new friend.

Amber nodded and led the group of people to the limo. As the limo drove off with the kids, the sounds of "Awesome" and "Wow" came from the others. However, the real surprise came when they entered into the gates of the palace.

The driver opened the door for them and the group exited and they were in awe at the size of the palace and it's beautiful appearance. The doors of the palace opened and out came Queen Renalia.

"Chris, Megan, Justin, Natalie, and Andrew, this is Queen Renalia," announced Amber.

Renalia gracefully walked down the steps and her dress shined in the sunlight. The group bowed and Renalia said, " I am pleased to meet you all. Any friend of Amber's is a friend of mine. Come, I will give you a personal tour of the palace and I will show you where your rooms will be."

The group followed the queen and still they questioned themselves if what they were seeing was real.

■   ■   ■   ■   ■   ■   ■   ■   ■   ■   ■   ■   ■   ■

The next three days went by really quickly and very soon the day came. Amber got butterflies in her stomach but she was too excited to even worry about that.

Once Amber was ready, she looked at herself in the mirror. She wore a beautiful dark green dress that went to the floor. She wore a necklace with an emerald in the center. Her earrings matched as well. The sleeves were long and her nails were painted a gold color. Her makeup looked perfect. Her hair was up in a decorative bun.

The queen entered and approached Amber saying, "Are you ready, Amber?"

"Definitely," she replied.

"I will meet you in the room where the coronation was held. One of my servants will let you know when you can come," said the queen leaving.

"I'd never imagine that I would be in any position like this. This is out of this world!" said Amber to herself.

A knock was heard at the door. It opened slightly and a young woman peeked through, "Miss Amber, it is time."

Amber nodded, exited the room and was led to the coronation room. Once she was at the door she could hear the chatter of people behind the closed doors. Suddenly the chatter ceased and the queen started talking. Amber couldn't hear what she was saying. Then the talking stopped and it was silent. The doors slowly opened and Amber knew that it was her cue to start walking in.

Everyone was amazed and they were all smiling. She was able to get a glimpse of her brother and friends over in the middle of the audience.

When Amber reached the queen she knelt and the queen said, "Amber Oak of the United States of America. I present to you this Medal of Honor, for your brave acts of heroism. I deem you Lady Amber."

Amber rose up and bowed to the queen, " Thank you, your Excellency. It is truly an honor."

As music began to play, the queen exited to the next room where the after party would be. Amber then followed, and then the audience exited the room. As always the food was incredible and the reception was extremely fun. For the rest of the evening they partied.

■ ■ ■ ■ ■ ■ ■ ■ ■ ■ ■ ■ ■ ■ ■ ■

The next day was a sad one for the time had come when Amber, her brother, and her friends had to depart from this beautiful country. The queen went along with Amber to give her a proper farewell.

"I am glad we were able to meet each other, Lady Amber. You are truly an amazing friend. Thank you once again for saving my country and myself," said the queen, giving Amber a hug.

"You're welcome. If there is anything else I can help you with, Renalia, please let me know," said Amber.

The queen nodded as Amber and her friends boarded the plane. Amber took a seat by the window and Chris sat by her. Amber waved a final good-bye to Renalia and the young queen waved back. As the plane took off Amber was relieved to be going back to her home.

Hours later, Amber looked out into the night sky and felt closer to the stars.

"Hey, Amber," said Chris.

"Yeah?"

"About what I said, before you left home. Do me a favor... don't ever stop solving mysteries," he replied as he drifted off to sleep.

"Well, maybe you're right, Chris..." started Amber, but it was too late for he was already fast asleep.

Amber looked back into the night sky and thought that Chris was right. She was good at solving mysteries. "I wonder what other mystery waits for me," said Amber to herself. Then she closed her eyes and went into her dream world once again.

The End

A Deadly Revenge - Part 1

Chapter 1

A Surprising Request

It was a cold, snowy December day in Ipswich, Massachusetts and Amber Oak was on her way to school. "Man! Why does it have to be so cold out?" she grumbled to herself.

The snowy landscape around her was beautiful! Snow draped off the trees and off in the distant, the sledding hill looked very inviting. Her toes started to freeze and her fingers became numb. Luckily, the faint glow of the high school came in the distance. She ran as fast as she could and got inside the warm, protective building. Slowly but surely her body warmed up head to toe. What a relief that was! As Amber walked to her locker, her friend, Jessie rushed up to her and said, "Amber! I've got some really great news!"

"What is it?" asked Amber, smiling as she put her books in her locker.

"There's a really, really cute foreign student here!" replied the excited girl.

"Where's he from?" asked Amber slightly curious.

"Galacia and he has the most adorable accent! His name is Jeffery!" continued Jessie.

"Jessie, I think you're overreacting," said Amber.

"Oh, yeah? Well, take a look, here he comes now," said Amber's friend with a giggle.

Amber turned around and saw a tall young man with light brown hair and blue eyes. She had to admit, Jeffery did look very handsome, but she had always thought that she was better off solo. Amber was kind of surprised, for he started walking toward her. Unfortunately some of the popular girls were tagging along.

"Hey Jeffery! This is Amber Oak," said Jessie.

"Wow, so you are Amber. I have heard a lot about you, good things of course," said Jeffery smiling and showing his gleaming white teeth.

Amber gave a slight smile and saw Jeffery shoo the other girls away.

"Good luck, Amber!" whispered Jessie with a giggle.

"Wait, Jessie!" exclaimed Amber.

Jeffery smiled at her when suddenly the bell rang.

"Hey, Amber do you mind if I walk you to your class?" asked Jeffery.

"Thanks, that's really nice of you, Jeffery," replied Amber slightly blushing.

"Please, call me Jeff, Jeffery just seems to formal," he replied.

Amber smiled and they started walking to Amber's class. As soon as they got there, Amber said bye.

Jeff stopped her and said, "Amber, I heard you are really good at solving mysteries! To tell you the truth, I love mysteries as well. I just wanted someone to teach me how to solve them which is why I wanted to meet you, that is, if it is not too much to ask.

Amber was shocked beyond belief. Nobody had ever asked her that!

"Wow! I'd love to!" said Amber smiling.

"I am glad you're accept my request. Let me know the place and the time and I will be available in a heartbeat. Here is my cell phone number," said Jeff, writing his number down.

"Will do!" said Amber still smiling.

Amber went into the classroom with a dazed expression on her face and for the rest of the day she wondered what she was going to teach him first.

Amber kept on pondering about this the whole day and even at lunch seemed more distant from her friends, until someone spoke up and said, "Amber! Hey! Earth to Amber!"

"Huh? What?" said Amber coming back to reality.

"I asked you how your day's been going," replied her friend.

"Oh sorry, Hunter! I guess I've been kind of in my own little world," replied Amber apologetically.

"Yeah, kind of noticed that," replied Hunter with a slight smile.

"Well, the answer to your question is, I'm perfectly fine!" said Amber with a daydream expression.

"Okay, who are you and what have you done with Amber?" asked Hunter with a hint of seriousness in his voice.

"What? Am I not allowed to be extremely happy for once in my life?" asked Amber with a smile.

"Not unless this "happiness" involves someone I don't know!" teased Hunter.

"Okay, okay you caught me!" said Amber.

"What? Me? Catch the greatest teen sleuth of all times?" laughed Hunter.

"Get real!" said Amber nudging Hunter, "All right, you know that new foreign student, Jeff?"

Hunter's joyful expression turned semi serious and he replied, "Oh great! Please tell me you're not falling for him?"

"No! Of course not! He just talked to me today and asked if I could train him on how to be a detective! Not only that, but he walked me to my classroom!" exclaimed Amber.

Hunter gave Amber a concerned look and felt her forehead then replied, "Amber, are you feeling okay?"

"Yeah, why?" she replied.

"Well, it's just that I've never seen this side of you!" said Hunter in a concerned tone.

"I'm fine. Don't worry, it's strictly teaching!" said Amber with a smile.

Just then the bell rang and just before Hunter and Amber departed to their classes Hunter said to Amber, "I hope that's all it is."

As Amber was walking to her class, she ran into Jeff.

"Hi Jeff! Hey, if you want to come by my place Saturday I'll text you the directions and we can start your training then," said Amber.

"That would be fantastic!" replied the handsome young man.

Amber quickly texted Jeff her address and they each set off for their own ways.

Chapter 2

The Training Begins

"So Amber, why was Hunter so upset?" asked Amber's friend, Jessie, as they walked to their buses.

"Beats me, I guess it started when I mentioned Jeff and how I was going to teach him how to be a detective," explained Amber.

"That would do it," replied Jessie.

Amber gave Jessie a questioning look and he replied, "Hunter doesn't like Jeff at all because to Hunter he takes Jeff as a threat. I know it's confusing but it's just plain jealousy.

Amber shrugged it off and went to her bus. To her surprise Jeff was there!

"Hey Jeff! I didn't know you were on my bus!" said Amber sitting down in the seat right next to him.

"Yeah, isn't that a coincidence!" exclaimed Jeff in shock. For the rest of the ride Amber and Jeff would not stop talking. They found out they had more in common then they had imagined! Unfortunately, the bus ride had come to a quicker end then they had anticipated.

"Well, I'll see you tomorrow!" said Amber as she got off the bus.

Amber walked inside the house and she found her brother, Chris, at the table working on his laptop.

"Hey kiddo! What's up?" asked Chris.

"Oh nothing," said Amber in a dreamy voice.

"Okay, what happened?" questioned Chris.

Amber told him the whole story.

"Wow! Sounds like my little sister has her first boyfriend!" said Chris.

"Cut it out! He's not my boyfriend!" replied Amber defensively, "I'm just teaching him how to be a good detective!"

"Yeah, likely story," laughed Chris, "Anyway just watch yourself, okay? You can never trust teen guys nowadays. I know, I was one!"

"I know, I know, you don't have to worry, Jeff's really kind," replied Amber.

"Hey, it's my job, Amber," replied her brother halfway serious.

Amber could hardly sleep that night. She was extremely excited. She just couldn't wait till Saturday.

The rest of the week went by really slow and Amber was working extremely hard to prepare for Saturday on top of studying for upcoming exams. In fact she almost stayed up all hours of the night preparing for everything! Unfortunately, her friends kept on teasing her about Jeff and not only that, Hunter seemed to be upset with her. She couldn't figure out why so she just brushed it off and assumed it to be a childish phase.

Finally the day came and Amber started cleaning the house like crazy.

She had been up since nine thirty in the morning, dusting, vacuuming, doing the laundry, cleaning her room, and doing the dishes, the whole nine yards! This in turn put Chris into a shock when he woke up to find the house spotless! When Amber looked at the clock it was one in the afternoon.

Suddenly the doorbell rang and Amber quickly put all of the cleaning supplies away and rushed to the door. She opened it and found Jeff smiling at her.

"Hi Jeff! I'm so glad you were able to make it!" exclaimed Amber, "Come on in!"

Jeff came in and took off his coat and followed Amber to the living room.

"So, what will you teach me first, Miss Detective?" asked Jeff.

Amber smiled and replied, "Well I'm going to first teach you the basics really, fingerprints, fingerprint dusting, but the major thing I'll go over is theft."

"That sounds great! I cannot wait to start!" said Jeff.

Amber smiled and started her teaching. Amber was teaching for a while now and lost track of time. Before either one of them knew it, it was seven p.m.!

"Oh man! I'm so sorry, Jeff! I didn't realize what time it was!" apologized Amber.

"Oh, do not worry, Amber! My dad does not mind that I am out this late. Hey, do you want to go out for dinner tonight? It will be my treat!" replied Jeff.

"Hold on, let me ask my brother!" said Amber rushing up the stairs.

Amber found her brother yet again working on his laptop, but this time he was in his room, sitting on his bed.

"Hey, Chris, Jeff offered to take me out to dinner, can I go?" asked Amber hastily.

"Wow, it's getting real serious real fast!" said Chris putting his laptop to the side and looking at Amber.

"No, it's not!" said Amber defensively, "he's just being kind."

"So how are you going to get to wherever you're going?" asked her brother seriously.

"I believe Jeff has a car," replied Amber honestly.

"Amber!" exclaimed Chris, "Are you sure it's wise to trust a guy you just met?"

"Chris! Chill out, will you? He's just a friend!" said Amber.

Chris took a deep breath and replied with reluctance, "Fine, you can go, just take your cell phone with you."

Amber smiled and gave her brother a huge hug. She then grabbed her cell phone from her charger and ran down the stairs.

"My brother said yes!" exclaimed Amber in obvious excitement.

"That is great. I just called my dad and he said it would be okay that I am out for a couple more hours," replied Jeff.

The two set off for the restaurant. While they were driving, Amber started to think, "Why was everyone so skittish when it comes to her and Jeff? It's not like he was hiding something from her."

Chapter 3

Complications

The dinner went great! Believe it or not, Amber was actually considering dating him! Weeks went by and Amber still trained Jeff until one day, Jeff wasn't able to make it! Amber was pretty upset for this was the big day. The day to test Jeff's knowledge and to see how well he learned. Amber had waited for Jeff to call, because he usually called her before coming over, but he never did! So Amber eventually ended up calling him.

"Hello?" said Jeff.

"Hey Jeff, it's me, Amber. Aren't you coming over today?"

"Oh man! That was today! Shoot! I forgot to call you and tell you that my dad and I had made other plans. I am so sorry. See, my dad and I were going to visit some friends today that we have not seen in quite some time. I feel so bad about all this," replied Jeff apologetically.

Amber was devastated but replied,

"It's okay, we'll do it some other time. Just let me know when you're free."

"Well, I am free tomorrow if you want to do it then," suggested Jeff.

Amber agreed and they said good-bye. For the rest of the day Amber seemed quite upset. She watched some mystery shows, called some friends, and read some books. One of the friends she called was Hunter. Unfortunately, he wasn't home. "He must be playing a video game or something," Amber thought to herself. The whole day went by really slow, for Amber was anticipating for the next day in hopes that nothing would again get in the way of her plans.

BEEP! BEEP! BEEP! BEEP! screamed Amber's alarm clock. Amber jumped up and realized that she had fallen asleep and had a terrible dream. She dreamt that she and

Jeff would get into some sort of quarrel. Amber quickly showered, got dressed, ate breakfast and brushed her teeth. Just as she was finishing, the phone rang and Amber picked it up.

"Hello?" said the sleuth.

"Hey, Amber, it is Jeff. Can I still come over?"

Amber got butterflies in her stomach and replied, "Sure, no problem."

Amber hung up and ran to the bathroom.

"There's got to be some make-up in here!" she exclaimed to herself.

After a couple minutes Amber came out and went to find her brother Chris.

"Hey Chris watchya up to?" asked the young sleuth.

"Oh I'm just working on..." said Chris, "Amber, are you wearing make-up?!"

Amber smiled and replied, "Yep!"

"I'll never understand you teen girls!" he mumbled under his breath.

DING-DONG!

"That's Jeff!" said Amber rushing down the stairs.

"Of course, who else would it be?" yelled Chris after her sarcastically.

Amber sprinted to the door and before she opened it she checked herself just to make sure she looked okay. Then calmly she opened the door and found Jeff standing there in the cold.

"Hey, come on in!" exclaimed Amber.

Jeff entered the warm comfortable house and took off his jacket.

"Okay, let us get started," said Jeff eagerly.

Amber was pleased of how excited he was to do the test.

Amber showed Jeff where the test was going to start and off he went. Amber watched Jeff carefully as he went from room to room gathering evidence to solve the test, which happened to be a huge mystery. Amber was actually quite impressed of how well he was doing. She knew Jeff had the brains to do it, just not the guts, for this mystery had some intense things added.

When the challenge ended Jeff came up to Amber with the solution to the mystery.

"Okay, so from what I have gathered, a man was murdered by his wife for she found out that he cheated on her with several other women. So she had a very good motive. Not only that, but her fingerprints were on the murder weapon! So am I right?" explained Jeff.

Amber was jaw-dropped. She had no idea he would be this good and solve the mystery so fast as well. This mystery took Amber over a month to put together and Jeff solved it within two hours!

"Jeff, I'm amazed. You truly are a great detective," replied Amber smiling.

"Well, I learned from the best!" said the handsome young man.

"Hey, let's go for a walk," suggested Amber blushing.

Jeff nodded and they set off for their walk.

As the two walked down a narrow path in the woods, Amber couldn't help noticing how beautiful the bare trees were. Their branches were covered in a thick layer of ice and when the sun was shining, the trees looked less than trees and more like gleaming crystals!

At the end of the trail, was a beautiful hand crafted wooden bench, and the two sat down.

"Hey, Amber, I really appreciate all you have done for me," said Jeff.

"It's not a problem, Jeff," replied Amber.

"I know this is very sudden, but all of the time we have spent together has made me realize that... I really do like you!" said Jeff staring into Amber's dark green eyes.

Amber's stomach had butterflies fluttering around again and she could have sworn her heart skipped a beat or two.

"I really like you, too," replied Amber.

"So... would you like to be my girlfriend?"

Amber felt like she was in heaven! How could this be? Not only was he extremely handsome, but he loved mysteries just like Amber. He was perfect! Amber thought he was the one!

"Amber?" asked Jeff, who now thought he offended her.

"Yes. My answer is a definite yes!" she replied.

"I am glad I have you for a girlfriend, Amber Oak!" said Jeff giving her a peck on the cheek.

Amber smiled and started to wonder if she was dreaming or was she somehow dead from one of her previous mysteries? Amber didn't know, all she did know was she was walking back down the trail hand in hand with the guy of her dreams.

The buzz about Amber and Jeff spread around the school like wildfire. Some people were really upset with the fact that Jeff was taken, mostly the girls that followed him. On the other hand Jessie, seemed really happy for Amber. Unfortunately, Hunter wasn't too happy, in fact he detested Jeff. He actually started to ignore Amber, but Amber didn't care, she had everything she had ever wanted!

Chapter 4

The Feud

"Well, I will see you later Amber! I have to stay after school," said Amber's boyfriend.

"Okay, well call me!" she replied.

Jeff kissed Amber on the lips and he then departed.

As Amber started for the bus she could feel someone watching her from somewhere. Amber looked around but saw no one. She must have been paranoid. But why? She had no reason to be, she had nothing to hide or to fear. The feeling drifted away as Amber continued walking. She then found out the reason for her abnormal paranoia, for out of the corner of her eye Amber saw Hunter and he had the sourest look on his face. Amber gave him a little smile and he returned a curt nod. They kept eye contact for a while until Hunter walked away. As she climbed the stairs to the bus she picked a seat and sat down. As Amber looked out the window the vision of Hunter's face kept reappearing in her mind. She just couldn't understand what she had done wrong! For the rest of the day and into the night the expression of Hunter's face flashed across her mind and into her dreams.

■ ■ ■ ■ ■ ■ ■ ■ ■ ■ ■ ■ ■

"Hey, hon!" greeted Jeff to Amber.

"Hi!" she replied back.

They talked the whole bus ride and even when they got to school. Amber put her things in her classroom and headed down the hall with Jeff hand in hand. Suddenly, Amber saw Hunter coming out of an English classroom.

"Hey Hunter! What's up?" asked Amber.

"Not much," he quickly replied.

"Hunter, can I talk to you? Alone?" asked Amber.

"Why would you want to talk to me?" replied Hunter.

"Well, you haven't been talking to me lately. Not only that but I've noticed you have been giving me nasty looks. So what's wrong?" explained Amber.

"I just think you're taking it a bit too seriously with Jeff. Personally I don't trust him and you shouldn't either," said Hunter.

"Give me one good reason!" exclaimed Amber getting angry.

"Well, for one I have some sources that tell me a lot about him and from what I know he has a pretty shady past," replied Hunter, " not only that, but he seems to me very temperamental."

"Wait, are you implying that you've been spying on him? I really can't believe you, Hunter!"

"No, Amber there's a perfectly good reason why I did this, I was worried about you," he replied innocently.

"Why?" questioned Amber, "Everyone else seems to be happy for us!"

"I guess I'm not everyone!" he shot back.

"No, Hunter, I think I know the real reason why you're so upset," replied Amber.

"Oh? Why?" asked Hunter.

Amber took a deep breath and replied, "You're just jealous!"

"WHAT? JEALOUS? ME? WHY WOULD I BE JEALOUS OF HIM? I MEAN, HE HAS TO DEAL WITH YOU!" he yelled back.

"Take that back!" screamed Amber almost in tears.

"Why should I take back the truth?" asked Hunter.

At this point Jeff overheard the feud and he walked over to Amber's side.

"What in the world is going on?" asked Jeff.

"Nothing, nothing at all," replied Hunter as he walked off in a hasty manner.

"Amber, are you all right?" asked Jeff looking into Amber's watery green eyes.

"I think I've lost a friend!" she replied.

Chapter 5

Terrifying Turns

Jeff comforted Amber that whole day. After a while Amber lightened up especially after Jeff invited her over for dinner.

■ ■ ■ ■ ■ ■ ■ ■ ■ ■ ■ ■ ■ ■

"Amber! You're not going!" exclaimed Chris cleaning up the kitchen.

"Oh and why not?!" replied the frustrated young sleuth.

"Anything could happen at his house, Amber," explained Chris.

" Ugh! Not you too! Chris, I'll make sure nothing happens. You can trust me, can't you?" asked Amber.

"You want the truth?" asked Chris.

Amber nodded.

"I'm honestly not sure. It seems to me like you're taking it too far with this boy that you hardly know anything about," said Amber's brother in a more calm tone.

"I know plenty about him, he's sweet, kind, caring, he makes me laugh even when he's not trying. He's honest, and more importantly he's a detective just like me!" said Amber in her day dreamy voice, "and he's not hiding anything!"

Chris stopped cleaning and sat down at the table. He motioned Amber to sit down as well and she did.

"Do you know anything about his past, though?" asked Chris.

"No, Jeff said he doesn't like to talk about it much," replied Amber.

"Doesn't that tell you something, Amber?" asked Chris.

"It tells me that my brother is to overprotective for his own good!" replied the girl.

Chris finally gave in and he let her go. Amber called up Jeff and he was on his way to pick her up.

Amber waited and waited and waited some more. Why was Jeff so late? Did he get into an accident? Amber started to worry now. Luckily, after a few moments Amber heard a vehicle pull up in the driveway. She rushed to the window and saw her boyfriend get out of his sleek, midnight blue sports car.

The doorbell rang and Amber went to greet Jeff.

"Hey babe, sorry that I was late, I had to pick up a few things for our dinner," said Jeff apologetically.

"No problem," said Amber smiling.

Amber got on her coat and shoes and the two headed out the door. As they were driving Amber said,

"I can't wait to see your dad, Jeff! So where does he work?"

"Oh… he works for a very top secret company that he does not want me to talk about, I can tell you that he is the head of the company," replied Jeff.

"That's cool. Are you planning to go into his business?" asked the curious sleuth.

"Actually, I am already in the business. My father personally trained me," replied Jeff.

"I hate to be nosy, but is it good pay?" asked Amber.

"Well, yes and no. See, it is also very confusing. You would not understand," said Jeff glancing at Amber.

"Here we are!" said Jeff pulling into a paved driveway. The house seemed quite large but also very ominous. There were trees that lined both sides of the driveway that gave off scary shadows on the ground below. As they got closer, Amber could see there were woods in the back.

"I like the house, it has a very creepy effect, but there are no lights on!" said Amber.

"Oh, my dad is the type of person who loves to conserve energy," said Jeff putting an arm around Amber.

Jeff and Amber reached the front door and they both stepped inside.

"So, where's your dad?" asked Amber.

"He is upstairs, come on I will show you," replied Jeff.

Amber followed him up the stairs and into a very bleak looking hallway. There wasn't much in there except a few boxes, which made Amber assume that they hadn't unpacked yet.

"He is in here," said Jeff opening a door.

Amber went in and she replied squinting, "I don't see him!" Amber turned around and her heart leapt when she saw Jeff lock the door.

"Jeff, what's going on?" asked Amber feeling her pocket just to make sure her pocket knife was there.

"You will soon see," said Jeff advancing toward Amber.

There was a bit of light from the moon reflecting in the room and Amber could see Jeff's menacing face coming toward her. Amber was able to catch a glimpse of what looked to be a dagger in Jeff's hand. At this point Amber was terrified. Jeff approached Amber and he said,

"Does this look familiar?"

Amber examined the dagger but it didn't look familiar to her at all. Amber replied, "No, should it?"

"Yes, it should. After all you did see this about three months ago, or so I have been told," replied Jeff with an intimidating look.

Amber gave him a questioning look, and Jeff replied in astonishment, "Wow, and you call yourself a detective. This should not be too difficult, Amber. Seriously, go back three months and think."

Amber gave him an offensive look; no one trashed her detective skills. Then she looked at the dagger again and a look of horror swept across her face, for she realized where this dagger had come from. She remembered one of her previous cases and remembered seeing that dagger in the hands of an infamous assassin who was the leader of an elusive assassin group called the Phantom Daggers. All she could remember of their encounter was the lead assassin, Roger, aiming his dagger at Amber. When she pieced the pieces together she then replied,

"Wait a second, you're Roger's son?"

"It took you long enough to figure it out!" replied Jeff.

"Wait, I didn't kill your father! It was Queen Renalia!" exclaimed Amber in defense.

"Yes, but if it was not for you, my father would still be alive. I mean, Queen Renalia only killed him out of protection of you. Plus, Princess Kaleya should have been Queen!"

"You are such a low life slug!" exclaimed Amber in a fury.

As soon as she said that, Jeff slapped her so hard that she fell to the ground. As she lay there, she could feel warm, sticky blood flowing from her nose. She looked up and stared Jeff down.

"YOU LIED TO ME!!!!" screamed Amber.

"Actually yes and no, I did lie to you but not about everything, I told the truth when I said that my father was the head of his business which happened to be the Phantom Daggers, and I am in my father's group. Oh I was also telling the truth when I said you would see my father," said Jeff holding up a little remote.

"What's that?" asked Amber.

"This is what I would call a little taste of revenge!" said Jeff walking out of the room and locking the door.

Amber tried to open the door with a pin she had in her pocket but it was no use. The only way to get out of that building was through the window.

Amber rushed over to it and looked out. She was on the second floor and the ground beneath looked everything but soft. It appeared to have a layer of ice covering it and beneath the ice was pavement.

Amber tried to open the window but there was no way it would open.

"There's gotta be a way out of here!" said Amber to herself.

Just as she said that, Amber heard an explosion coming from the hallway.

Suddenly, an orange glow came through the cracks of the door and the smell of fire reached its way into Amber's nose. Amber had to act quickly for if she didn't, she would be killed.

Chapter 6

A Hero in the Night

Amber looked around the room to try to find something to break the window. At this point it was her only way out. Amber searched the room and her eyes came upon a doorstopper near where the orange glow came from. Amber made a quick dash for the object. Suddenly, the fire reached the door and the flames crawled up it.

When Amber reached for the doorstopper a flame made its way to her hand. Amber didn't realize how close she was until she felt an immense, burning sensation on her hand and wrist. Amber quickly got her hand out of the fire's path and grabbed the doorstopper with her other hand.

She rushed to the window but as soon as she did that the entire room was engulfed with flames.

"Man! He must have had this place rigged somehow in order for the fire to spread this fast!" thought Amber.

Amber knew that it was only a matter of time before the floor she was on would collapse.

With much pain, Amber lifted the heavy doorstop and threw it at the window and broke the glass. The opening was just large enough for Amber to get through. The only thing the young detective was concerned about was if Jeff had heard the glass shatter. At this point Amber didn't care. If she was face to face fighting Jeff she was absolutely sure she would win. After all, she did take on many highly trained assassins and won!

Amber looked at the ground below. She thought for sure that if she'd jump she'd surely be dead and Jeff would've accomplished what he wanted. Yet, Amber only had two options. It was to either suffer and burn to death or jump and instantly die, well depending on how she landed. Amber took a chance and jumped out of the window.

She miraculously landed on the hard icy ground alive! Luckily she had jumped just in time, for the floor she had jumped from had collapsed.

Amber could hear sirens coming and knew that help was on the way. The teen detective attempted to get up but had collapsed when pain shot up her leg. Amber tried to move it but it was very painful. She assumed that it wasn't a break but it might be sprained badly and would need some attention.

Amber knew she had to get up for she was afraid that Jeff would still be around.

The girl's fear came true; she looked around and saw Jeff running toward her with his father's dagger in hand.

She got up as quickly as she could. Even though pain came to her every move she made, she had no other option if she wanted to survive!

Amber limped toward the woods behind the burning house as fast as she could. She made her way through many bushes, trees, and thorns with great difficulty. A couple times she was tempted to stop but she decided otherwise when she heard Jeff's footsteps behind her.

"You will die, Amber Oak!" yelled Jeff.

When Amber heard that, her heart leapt and she rushed through the thick wood faster.

Deep down inside she realized that Jeff wouldn't stop till she was dead. Suddenly, Amber came upon a raging river. This was it. Amber had to make another choice and soon. Would she jump into the perilous, deafening river or would she wait and take on Jeff with all the strength she had left?

Amber wasn't quick enough to decide; she suddenly felt the coldness of a razor-sharp dagger pressed gently against her throat. Amber tried to grasp her knife but Jeff had reflexes like a cat and seized her hand, which happened to be the wounded one.

Amber yelped in pain. Jeff still held Amber's damaged hand and with it he swung her around and threw her to the ground. Jeff raised his dagger and started to slash at Amber. The wounded girl attempted to fight back but Jeff was too powerful. At this point Amber knew she was as good as dead.

"Say good bye, Amber Oak!" exclaimed Jeff with the dagger raised.

Just as Amber thought she was done for, another person came and attacked Jeff! Who could this hero be? Amber couldn't really tell, mostly because she was semi-conscious and the fact that the two were fighting each other in the darkness made the scene very blurry.

But to her astonishment Jeff fell down! He appeared to be severely injured.

The hero hurried over to Amber. Amber moved back a bit but the hero said to her, "Amber, you'll be okay. I'll get you to the hospital!"

Amber still didn't know who this person was. The voice sounded very familiar, but she still couldn't match the voice.

"Amber, please, try to stay awake!" pleaded the hero.

Amber tried to, but she was too weak she just had to shut her eyes, just for a moment.

▪ ▪ ▪ ▪ ▪ ▪ ▪ ▪ ▪ ▪ ▪ ▪ ▪ ▪ ▪

Amber could hear voices. Was she dead? No she couldn't have been, these voices sounded familiar.

Amber's eyes flickered open. Where was she? There was a white ceiling, white walls and a bed with guardrails! It looked to be a hospital. Amber looked around and was relieved to see a familiar face it was Chris!

"Hey kiddo! Glad to see you awake!" exclaimed her brother.

Amber smiled and looked at her wounds. Her burned hand was bandaged and her leg was in a cast. Apparently the doctors thought it was broken. With all the running Amber did last night it didn't surprise her.

She had a few other wounds but they were minor.

"How did I get here?" asked Amber.

"Well, I'll let your hero explain!" replied Chris.

Chris motioned for someone to come in and to Amber's surprise her hero turned out to be Hunter!

"I'm gonna go get some coffee," said Chris. He knew of the feud between Hunter and Amber and he thought it'd be better if they could talk alone.

"Hunter! You saved me? Why? I mean I yelled at you and..." said Amber in total shock.

Hunter stopped her and explained,

"Yes, I know you yelled at me and of course I was mad for awhile, but I realized that something in my gut told me that I should still keep an eye on you no matter what. I decided to do some research on Jeff and I found out that he was the son of Roger, the famous assassin. I knew you were in terrible danger because I saw on the Internet that you were partially the cause of Roger's death. I pieced the puzzle together and I decided to go to your house and warn you, but I was too late! When Chris told me about your dinner date, I knew Jeff would try to kill you. I quickly told Chris and he called the police and I asked him if he knew where Jeff lived. Chris told me and I made my way to there. When I got there, I saw the place in flames. I saw you jump out of the window. When I saw that, I was petrified. I thought for sure you'd be dead, but when I saw you get up I was relieved. I was about to go help you but then I saw Jeff coming at you. I knew that was my cue to follow him. I tried to keep up with you but at times I got lost. When I finally caught up to you two, I saw him raise his dagger. I then attacked him. I pretty much beat him up. When I was done he was unconscious. I ran over to you and you were bleeding a heck of a lot. I carried you out of the woods. Your brother saw you and he pointed me to where the ambulance was. I carried you there and they took you away. I told the police where Jeff was and that he was unconscious when I left him. After that, I went with your brother in the ambulance and I've been here since."

"I just have one question," said Amber, "I yelled at you and everything, yet you still helped me? Why?"

"Amber, friends have their fights. Sure, ours was huge, but friends stick together," said Hunter.

Just then, Chris came in and he didn't look too happy.

"Chris, what happened?" asked Hunter.

"I got some news from the police. They said when they got to the location of where Jeff was, he was gone!"

Amber got shivers up her spine. The killer was still out there somewhere and Amber knew he wouldn't stop until he finished what he came to do!

To Be Continued...